UNDONE

C. BORDEN

Undone

Copyright © 2024 by C. Borden

All rights reserved

No part of this book may be reproduced in any form or by any electronic or mechanical means, including information storage and retrieval systems, without written permission from the author, except for the use of brief quotations in a book review.

Genre(s): *Science Fiction / Horror / Post-apocalyptic*

Published by C.B. Writing Solutions

Cover Art by C.B. Writing Solutions

Editing by InKarakter Author Services

Proofreading by C.B. Writing Solutions

Undone is a work of fiction. All names, characters, places, events, and incidents in this book are either the product of the author's imagination or used in a fictitious manner. Any resemblance to actual persons, living or dead, or actual events is purely coincidental.

AI Disclaimer – Absolutely no part of this book was created using generative-AI, to include content and cover. Additionally, no part of this book – not content, nor cover, nor any other aspect of this book in any of its formats – may be used for generative-AI without express permission from the author.

Even in the end, there is hope.

CONTENTS

Prologue	1
Chapter 1	7
Chapter 2	16
Chapter 3	28
Chapter 4	38
Chapter 5	47
Chapter 6	57
Chapter 7	66
Chapter 8	80
Chapter 9	89
Chapter 10	103
Chapter 11	115
Chapter 12	127
Chapter 13	138
Chapter 14	147
Chapter 15	157
Chapter 16	168
Chapter 17	176
Epilogue	189
Dear Reader	193
About the Author	195
Also by C. Borden	197

PROLOGUE

CHAOS REIGNED while alarms within the complex blared. The lab techs ran into the pressurized chamber and tore off their protective suits, taking care to wrap the booties, gloves, and masks within the discarded suits. They threw the contaminated bundles into the incinerator, then stood naked under the chemical bath, spitting, and sputtering as the chemicals burned the sensitive areas of their bodies.

After three full minutes under the harsh agents, they moved into the next chamber. Brilliant bursts of hot white light flashed at them from every angle to further cleanse their bodies of any microbes, germs, bacteria, or viruses that might have survived.

Finally, they moved into the third chamber and looked through a thick glass wall at the lab techs on the other side. With a loud hissing sound, a drawer slid out of the wall.

One tech stepped forward and pulled out three sets of scrubs. He handed them to the other two techs, carefully averting his gaze to give his female counterparts a measure of respect as they stood uncomfortable in their nakedness. The three quickly dressed and sat heavily on pull-out benches.

"Damn!" murmured one tech.

"What the hell happened in there?" a disembodied voice echoed over an intercom.

The male tech moved to the intercom and pushed a button. He glanced at the other two techs and grimaced.

"Experiment 25 happened. The last subject broke its bonds and tore Lieutenant Brown's suit."

"What of the subject? Is it viable?"

The male tech lowered his head as though struggling with his emotions. Then he looked up and spoke into the comm. "No. We had to kill it. We also had to restrain Dr. Vikalis."

"She was...?"

"The subject attacked her first. It bit clear through her suit and broke her skin."

The intercom went dead. The tech turned to the others.

"Lieutenant Brown, you are certain it did not break the skin?" he asked her.

She lifted her arm and turned it so the other two could see clearly. There was redness that promised bruising later, but no broken skin.

The other two relaxed visibly.

"What about you, Captain Hun?"

The other lab tech shook her head. "I'm fine. Shaken up. Did you see its eyes? It was dead. Completely. So how on earth was it able to attack?"

The male tech shook his head. "Beats me. I've never seen anything like it. What was Vikalis working on?"

The intercom crackled to life.

"We will pass in some MREs and water for the three of you. You'll stay in quarantine for the next twenty-four hours. During this time, one of you will need to go back into the lab and check on Dr. Vikalis. We need clinical data on how quickly her symptoms start."

One of the techs grumbled about having to eat one of the Military Ready-to-eat Meals, while Captain Hun moved to the intercom. "We do not have to do anything until someone explains to us what the hell we are working with in there. That subject was dead! There is no way..."

"You have your orders, Captain. Check in with us in two hours."

The intercom went quiet again. The three stared at each other in silence.

Major Hicklin frowned as he stared at the monitors displaying the lab and quarantine chamber. He glanced at the bank of monitors that showed the vital signs of the lab technicians.

So far, none of the three were showing signs of infection, but he had to assume they were already affected as well.

Protocol dictated to assume the worst. Twenty-four hours would be the determiner.

He slammed his hands down on the console.

"Shit!"

When he regained his composure, he stared at the screen that showed Dr. Vikalis, strapped to the table. While they could not get her vitals, it was clear that she was suffering at an increased rate. Major Hicklin noted she was sweating, and her eyes seemed jaundiced. He wished he could get some better readings on her, but the lab techs, just reservists on their weekend duty to fulfill their reserve contracts, were justifiably scared to return to the lab. He was in no hurry to fill out more incident reports should one of them get bit.

Another monitor revealed Experiment 25's body on the floor, struck in the head with chilling accuracy by the master sergeant. The major noted the death blow in his notebook, too.

When the intercom buzzed, his gaze flew back to the monitors; particularly the monitors for the chamber. All seemed well for the time being, except for Captain Hun, who pounded on the button as she stared through the glass doors of the partitions leading back to the lab.

"Major... Do you see this?" she asked, her voice shaky.

He looked at the monitor and watched the doctor convulsing violently.

"I see it," he responded. "There is nothing we can do."

"Do you still want us to get samples?" the captain asked with a hesitant voice.

The major sat in silence as he debated for a few minutes.

"No. Let's just clear you three. Then we will call in the regular crew to take over."

He watched the monitor as the captain visibly relaxed and nodded.

"Thank you, Sir."

The major did not reply. He sat back and watched the techs on the screens. He prayed for forgiveness, suspecting he would not be able to release the three reservists.

The major assumed the worst but had no way of knowing that the virus was not just one virus, but two. They existed together, fighting for survival. The original was transmitted through transferring body fluids through bites or scratches. The other, a near identical copy, was spread through air. Even after a twenty-four-hour quarantine, the airborne virus was not yet apparent. They had no way to test for it and relied solely on the appearance of visual signs and symptoms. They did not know all three reservists had it. The lieutenant got it when her suit was compromised. The other two techs when they were confined in the chamber with her for those twenty-four hours.

Major Hicklin knew the gestation period for the original virus. It had been developed and grown in that very lab as an agent to battle a similar virus generated by the Chinese. That first virus was not supposed to kill its infected. It was intended to kill only bio-engineered, genetic viruses like itself. Instead, to his horror, it attacked the host's brain, changing its chemical make-up and turning off certain brain centers while amplifying others. In every subject, including Doctor Vikalis, the virus killed everything in the body except for a small part of the brain. The only signs of life that the otherwise dead subjects exhibited were those instincts of insatiable hunger and unrelenting rage.

By the time the major realized the virus had mutated and left the confines of their ultra-secure facility, the entire eastern seaboard reported sick, dying, and dead rising. Sadly, when he documented his mistake, he had already contracted the infection and spread it to dozens of his subordinates.

Four days after he noted his symptoms, alone in a lab full of dead, dying, and reanimated, he put a gun to his head. With tears spilling down his cheeks, he pulled the trigger, hoping his wife would someday forgive him for leaving her in a world full of monsters he helped create.

CHAPTER ONE

THE VOICES, the rage, the confusing madness - it was all gone.

There was only silence.

Deafening silence, which was even worse. I could reflect on my madness. My unspeakable acts. I could see the faces. The bodies. All the humans I slaughtered or turned.

Humans have a word for what I felt. Guilt, I think. It seemed impossible. I wasn't capable of that, or any other feeling.

No. I could think. I couldn't *feel*. Wrong. I could feel red. And black. Worse, I saw red.

Though less when the silence took over.

The new silence was driving me mad. I had traded one madness for another and found myself getting lost in the past. Broken memories of a time I vaguely recalled as being human resurfaced.

Humans thought we were stupid. They thought we were mindless monsters with only one goal in mind: killing—feeding—killing—one and the same. That was true, of course. But we were so much more, too. If they knew that only the madness kept us from organizing our thoughts and acting on our knowledge, they would be even more horrified.

We knew it was a human-made pathogen that turned the world upside down. We knew, but the rage and hunger made us incapable of doing anything beyond satisfying our instincts.

We knew the pathogen was intended to battle another pathogen. The precedent had been set a decade earlier. When a pathogen like this one first surfaced, back in the 2020s, it killed millions. It had been created in China to help control population growth. But that one crossed the world. It was successful for the elite hoping to kill the elderly and sickly. It was successful for greedy corporations that sold vaccines against pathogens. But that first one was not the last. It proved to be an effective tool in the world governments' ability to manage their populations.

Thus, more pathogens were developed with the same goal in mind: population control and corporate greed. Most were made in those countries that were more lax on regulation. Each pathogen was more dangerous than the last.

The final one was created not for population control, but for eradication of China's enemies. Some remote labs got their hands on that most recent engineered virus and tried to create cures.

All failed.

The humans never considered that the pathogen would mutate, spread, and move beyond their reach within hours of dissemination. None of their horror movies prepared them for the apocalypse that hit the planet within days of their tests.

There was no stopping it. No way to cure it. It was hard to kill. The few who could have done it soon became monsters of their own making, or ended their own lives before the monster took over.

Even as monsters, we could remember that.

I could remember.

But in the madness, all I could focus on was the drive to rip, tear, and feed. When I wasn't doing that, I wandered about, lost in the never-ending madness of the past.

Human population dropped quickly while our numbers grew steadily.

When the pathogen stopped turning them, we took over. Our numbers grew so much that it became harder and harder to find humans to feed on. We fed on anything we could find- including each other. Little affected how we moved about so long as we found food and something to take the rage out on.

I was one of them.

I am different now.

The monsters I walked with sensed it. But instead of attacking me, taking out their rage on me, they avoided me. I wandered among my kind, the product of madness and desperation, but I was no longer mad or desperate.

In the weeks that the madness left my mind, I stumbled across another whose madness had quieted. While I expected the creature to avoid me, it got so close I could smell its rancid breath. The two of us stood there staring each other down, waiting for the other to make the first move. Finally, as if by mutual agreement, it went one way, while I went the other. As it wandered through the group, I noticed the other zombies avoided it, too.

Maybe I should have followed it. After all, it was more like me than the zombies I was with.

There were no more voices. No more burning rage directing me which path to take, and I didn't know what to do.

There I was, with the infuriating silence in my head. The others seemed ever more alarmed by my presence. Still, they didn't react to me the way they did to the rare humans we encountered. I think they expected me to snap out of this state, whatever it was. If they thought about my difference at all.

I think they were even more alarmed because I was not thrown into the same fits of rage as they were. If one of us caught the scent of food, it would awaken our thirst and rage, driving us all into the same frenzy.

Not me. Not anymore.

———

One morning, as the sun rose over the distant hills I, like the others, caught the scent of flesh. Flesh mingled with fear. A salty, coppery smell. Overwhelming. Triggering.

We were all familiar with it. It was the scent of a human. As I scanned the area from where the smell blew from, I stayed still while all hell broke loose around me. The others screamed, clawed at the ground or each other, and lifted their faces into the breeze to better decide which way to run and find that human meal.

As I stood there, one of the undead noticed me. Fury drove it into my face. Again, I stood unmoved. I knew the hazard I was facing. Yet, I felt nothing. I did not feel the instinct to flinch, to run, to survive. I simply stood there as it waved its gray, rotten arms and hands and sputtered a gory spittle in my face, with its lifeless gaze boring into my own.

I stood there. The silence in my head offered no advice, no direction. Somehow, I knew I should react. Yet, I could not recall why.

Finally, hunger overcame the other. It jerked away from me and propelled toward the smell that promised food and outlet. The rest of the group followed, ambling along at different speeds, their gaits determined by the damage done in the transformation from human to monster.

The size of the unfortunate human being tracked would not matter. Our hunger was easily sated with a few small nibbles. As far as food went, a single human could feed a group three or four times the size of the group I was with, but that human would only be a source of food until it underwent the change. The newly turned would be the fastest and strongest for a while. Until another human was found.

I ambled along after the group.

I felt no hunger.

I felt no rage.

I just followed, because that was all I could think of doing. I wandered to the edge of the raging pile of creatures. They crawled over each other to get to the screaming human underneath. I could hear death: the tearing of clothes, the wet sucking of flesh as it tore. Screams turned into whimpers, moans, and finally gurgling. The human died choking on its own gore.

Still, the tearing, grabbing, and raking went on as the group fought each other to get to the fresh meat. When, finally, the group's collective hunger was sated, the mass moved away from the body.

I moved in to stare down at what was left. I still felt no hunger, but a tickle at the edges of my mind told me I needed to eat.

I examined the mess before me. Remnants of a bright t-shirt under a heavy jacket. Torn blue jeans. Heavy boots with holes worn through the soles. A hat covered most of the face. I squatted down next to the human body and pushed back the hat. Man or woman, I could not tell from what was left of the face. Nothing about the clothing gave away its gender. Even through the holes in the clothing, this human was androgynous.

With no rage guiding my hand, I reached out. Suddenly tentative, I grasped at the flesh from one arm. It came away with a spray of blood.

As I squatted there and ate of the flesh, I watched the human for signs of the change. With some, it happened fast. Others seemed to take a long time. The longest I could remember took almost a complete day.

This one changed fast. Before my eyes, the skin turned different shades of green and gray. The short-cut blonde hair under the hat seemed to turn ragged and lackluster. The open eyes staring into the daytime sky changed from the color of the grass on which it lay to a deep burgundy with points of black, the irises fully dilated. As the irises changed, I stood up and moved back toward the group that now walked idly and in indeterminable patterns several paces from the body.

Some of the others looked at me as I approached. They still did nothing, neither accepting me nor condemning me. I clutched the flesh from the arm in my hands. Returning to a squatting position, I gnawed on the flesh and watched the transformation before me.

This was the first one since my silent madness began.

An unfamiliar sensation crept over me as the human turning monster showed more obvious signs of its dreadful change. Patches of sickly green flesh edged gaping wounds, not healing them, but effectively stopping the fast rot that should have occurred naturally.

I wondered if the humans studied that fact. Our bodies repaired themselves, differently than human bodies repaired themselves, I was certain, but still, they did and for no reason that I could understand. The fleshy wound where I had taken a piece from the arm was soon covered in the sickly green-gray flesh my kind was known for. The face seemed to put itself together, though I was certain it was still no good representation of what the human looked like before it had been attacked.

A sudden desire to be the first next time we came across a human took hold of me. I wanted to see a human with my quiet, unclouded mind. I could not help but wonder if seeing a human without feeling the rage would make a difference.

The physical transformation complete, the new monster's body convulsed for a while. When the seizures stopped, the creature vaulted from the ground as if drawn by the strings of a puppet master. Strange cracking noises came from it as it moved its arms, neck, and legs. Slowly, it turned its gaze toward our group.

It launched itself in our direction. Complete chaos took over for several minutes as the new addition to the group showed its strength and speed by tossing several of us around the area with little effort.

As I still squatted to the side of the group, it noticed me. Maybe it caught the scent of its old flesh. It ran in my direction and stopped just short of me. It smelled me; smelled the flesh in my hands. Then it reached out tentatively.

Strange. It seemed afraid of me.

I remained squatting, which forced it to squat as well. As it sat before me, I sensed something I had not noticed before in any of the others. There was clarity and realization behind the stare. Shrouded and distant, but it was there.

Were we all like this, I wondered. When we first changed, did we keep a small piece of our human selves for just a while before the madness took over?

The new undead thing grabbed my face and stared into my eyes. I saw terror and a plea. A plea to be killed. In that instant, I knew what it wanted. And I knew I could do it if I was faster than the madness sure to take its mind.

Dropping my pound of flesh, I grabbed the creature's head between my hands. I gripped it tightly, expecting the creature to buckle, kick, scratch, and fight.

It did not.

I stared back into its still pleading eyes as I squeezed. With a loud pop, I crushed its skull and brain.

A human would have died instantly. One of us, not so much. It was certain death for us, but not a fast one. I watched the rage turn to acceptance. The acceptance turned to something else I could not place. I held its head in my hands, supporting its entire body in that awkward squatting position until the pupils returned to a normal size. To my surprise, the irises returned to their original shockingly green color.

At that moment, a wave of something unfamiliar washed over me.

What was it? Feeling? Emotion?

Startled, I dropped the corpse and backed away. I stared at the dead human; a dead thing like me. As that strangeness took hold of me, other sensations gripped me. The next thing I knew, I was ambling away from the horde.

I didn't even know why.

CHAPTER TWO

ONE THING my kind was not so good at was sensing the passing of time. We recognized long versus short spans of time, but without obvious changes such as day turning to night, we didn't care about or fathom its passing.

When I left, I was not aware of the time of day. I couldn't tell how long I walked for. I simply did. My body did not tire easily. Even with the changes in my mind, my body still seemed unaffected. I did not get out of breath. I didn't breathe. My muscles did not burn from exertion. My body kept moving as I fought and feared the things in my mind.

I could not erase the image of the creature I just killed. Why did it bother me so much?

As day turned into night, I kept moving. I crossed barren fields long left farrow, full of weeds and tree saplings, as forests were encroaching back into areas humans had long since destroyed. I moved through a large forest and emerged on the other side, forced to stop at the edge of a swiftly roaring river.

Pulling up short, I realized it was the middle of the night, with a full moon overhead. My instincts told me I was extremely far away from the group I had been traveling with.

Part of me wanted to return.

I had never been alone before. At least, not since becoming this monster.

Alone.

We were never alone. I was never alone. Always in groups of at least three, we were more effective hunters.

Nagging snippets, images of a past long gone, raced through the silence in my head. I feared. More than that, I understood what I was feeling, even though it was new to me. It was not mere caution. It was deeper. Darker.

I knew caution. I experienced that even in my madness. We were cautious about humans. Humans could destroy us, but we often simply overpowered them. Our sheer numbers, combined with our ferocity, fearlessness, and madness, did not give humans much chance to do anything except flee before us. They rarely predicted our presence. They certainly could not predict our actions. So, despite their rational ability to destroy every one of us, they were unable to do so.

Still, they were the only living beings who could truly harm us if they could rally the numbers. So even in madness, we were cautious with them.

No. What I felt there at the side of the river, as I realized I was alone, was not caution. It was fear. It was an uncomfortable cold feeling that started in the back of my mind, a low hum between my rotten ears. The more I tried to tune it out, like I always tried to do with the raging voices, the more intense the feeling became. The fear grew. I looked about me terrified by my loneliness.

Yet, as I stood there with night changing to day, faint sounds reached me. There were humans nearby.

I listened to the noises they made. There were a lot of them. Much more than I ever heard together at once before. The noise they made added caution to this new feeling of fear.

Humans typically tried to be quiet, so they wouldn't attract our attention. This group, however, did not seem afraid of attracting my kind. Being so close to humans that were not afraid of being heard deepened my caution.

However, their fearlessness also made me curious. In the end, curiosity got the better of me. As I stood listening, I had a choice to make. I'm not sure how long I stood there before I decided to observe these humans. Slowly, I made my way toward them.

Their camp was just over a hill. After I crested that hill, I stood behind a tree, not ready to reveal myself. Part of me expected the humans would react in terror. But now, an unknown part of me was not so sure. That part wondered if they would be able to sense the change in me. If they did, how would they respond to my presence?

Now that rage no longer drove me, I wondered what it would be like to be among the humans. Supposing I could get close enough, I knew they would probably attack and try to destroy me, rather than take the time to realize I was alone, and different. So, I stood behind the tree and decided to just watch.

The camp was haphazard. Tents and beat-up vehicles were scattered around in no clear order. Campfires still blazed near many of the tents. People huddled around the fires. Several armed men walked the perimeter. They hollered back and forth to each other in obvious disregard for any of my kind that might be nearby. Their brazenness astonished me.

As I watched the men walk around the camp, I caught a whiff of the other group members' scent carried by the wind. It was a diverse group. There were men and women, both young and old. I could even tell the difference between the races by the scent of their sweat. I could taste it in the air.

The human species was, indeed, an incredible kaleidoscope of appearance, smell, and sound. Yet they all tasted the same. I cringed. Sudden disgust with the hunger that pushed its way to the front of my mind made me shudder.

Surprisingly, there was a scent I could not place. It was human, but not a smell I had come across before. There was something clean about it. Pure, and accompanied by a strange sound. A constant, high-pitched wailing. Demanding. Scared. Hungry?

The strange scent woke something in me. It compelled me to move forward.

As I moved away from the safety of the tree line and stumbled down the hill toward the camp, I realized I was about to die. Still, I moved forward, expecting the men with the guns to shoot me down. They would see me as a monster. They would think I came to destroy them. No other possibility would ever cross their minds.

A guard saw me. He let out a shrill whistle and alerted the other guards. The men whistled back-and-forth. Other people grabbed guns as well and rushed to the perimeter of the camp. Strangely, the fear I felt before disappeared. It was replaced by a new feeling; another one I was not familiar with. This new feeling drove me forward. It compelled me to look. To truly look in the eyes of the humans before me, even though the unusual smell and sounds baffled me.

The humans leveled their guns at my head, taking careful aim to protect themselves from me. I slowed down, but I made eye contact with the human closest to me. Unable to stop myself, I continued toward the group. I hoped the human realized I was different.

Guns cocked. The humans' voices raised in alarm. Confusion, mingled with anxiety, tinged their voices: after all, I was alone.

The human staring back at me cocked his head to one side. There was wisdom in his appraisal. He watched me, his gaze roaming from my head to my feet. Then, he stared into my face. Into my eyes.

Behind him, the source of the smell and sound revealed itself. It was wrapped in a bundle, held by a scared-looking woman. It was a tiny human. A baby. I stared in its direction, trying to make out what the tiny human looked like, but it was too carefully bundled. All I would get was its smell and sound.

As though sensing my interest, it finally fell quiet. The woman that held it disappeared into a tent, and the scent disappeared from the breeze.

I shifted and looked back at the one man who was still watching me.

Without warning, the man lifted his gun up in the air, yelling at the top of his voice. He got every person's attention. While their guns were still pointed at me, they were now focused on him.

He spoke excitedly to the group of people. An argument arose. The guardsmen gestured excitedly at me, their voices thick with anger. One man, the one who had first seen me, got in the other man's face and yelled repeatedly. Meanwhile, the man I made eye contact with refused to back down.

Finally, he broke from the group and marched toward me. He marched toward me with his gun in hand and made eye contact with me again. Dread settled in my mind and warned me to go back to my kind, but as the man held my stare, I could not bring myself to turn away.

―――

Time stood still, but the man still stared up at me. Sounds came from his mouth. Sounds I would have understood once upon a time. Now, despite being able to think, despite all the knowledge I retained from my old life, I could not understand.

Cocking my head to the side, I tried to make my mouth move the same way his did. I tried to make the sounds he was making.

When finally, a sound escaped my mouth, it was not the same. The man stepped backward, squinting, his forehead wrinkling up strangely. Behind him, another man approached, larger than the first but with a menacing glare on his face. It was the same man the first man had been fighting with.

The taller man stepped close to me. He pulled a weapon from his belt and raised it to my face. He pressed the gun to my temple. Anger flashed in his eyes. No. Not anger. What I saw in his glare was familiar.

Rage. Hate. I knew those. I recognized them, though I didn't feel them anymore. But I knew still them.

I stood still and waited.

The first man stepped between us. Shockingly, he reached down and grabbed my hand. He held it up for the other man to look at. He pointed at a part of my hand, and ran a finger along it, making the other man look at it too. Not understanding, I also looked.

Huh.

How had I not noticed that before?

The curious man pointed to and touched a patch of skin on my hand. It was not gray. The small patch of skin didn't look dead. It looked more like the man's skin, though it was not the same color. His skin was pink and plump, and suddenly a pang of hunger surged through me.

I yanked my hand away so I could look at it more closely. It was tinged blue. Not rotten, but also not human. I backed away from the men as I stared at my hand. The angry man instantly stepped forward, pressing the point of his gun back to my head. I stopped. Stood still.

The other man called something back to the crowd. The crowd seemed to shift and sway before it divided. A woman emerged. She looked at me first, then at both men next. After a moment, she came forward slowly.

As she approached, the noises coming from her mouth were demanding and afraid yet determined.

The first man turned back to me, waving in my face, pulling my attention back to him. He pointed at my hand. Making motions, he expressed he wanted to show it to the woman.

I looked back at her. She stood behind the two men, keeping a safe distance.

Watching her, I slowly raised my hand. The man with the gun pressed his weapon harder, so I had to lean my head to the side a little. The pressure didn't hurt, but I lacked the strength to push back against it.

Suddenly, I realized I needed to eat. I bit my lip. The woman gasped and turned white. I guess I bit into my lip. It happens. We don't feel pain. We just know when we are being destroyed. But knowing and feeling are two different things.

The first man made more sounds at the second man, until he withdrew his gun. Though, as he did, he made a lot of angry noises, pointing at the first man, then at me in such an agitated way, I wondered why the gun didn't go off.

The first man took my hand and held it up for the woman to see. She leaned between the two men to get a closer look. Lifting a hand to cover her nose, she leaned closer over my hand. She snapped upright.

What was that expression? Her eyes were wide. Mouth open. No sounds escaped. She looked at me, then at the first man. She nodded and turned back to the camp.

The first man made sounds at the other man, who pressed his gun back to my head and pushed. I looked at the one who had seemed to be curious about me, and saw he was more agitated.

Were they going to destroy me now?

But the first man made more sounds at me. He stepped away from me and waved his arm. He took another step and waved at me repeatedly. Meanwhile, the man with the gun started to push me toward the first man.

Then, it clicked. The first man wanted me to follow him.

Though I was not sure why, I complied.

I followed him closer to the camp. Before we got into the camp, however, he diverted to the side. There, at the side of the camp, on the back of one of the beat-up vehicles, sat a large box.

He opened it, pulled down a block, and pointed at me. Then he pointed at the box.

With dread, I realized they didn't want to destroy me. Worse. They wanted to cage me.

I stopped.

The man with the gun pressed the point into my head, forcing me to bend forward, but I did not move my legs.

I watched the first man. He swung his arms around. He looked upset with the second man. Finally, the taller man stepped back. The gun was still level with my head, but he gave me room to move.

The first man pointed at me, then at the large metal box. Curious, I stepped closer. Inside, the box was dark. That didn't bother me. Light or dark. That did not scare me.

Scared.

That new, yet strangely familiar feeling resurfaced.

I was scared.

I stepped backward and looking around me.

The man with the gun was moving his mouth. The sounds emerging were sharp and loud. He made those sounds at me, waving the gun with one hand, and pointing at the box with the other.

The first man stepped up to me.

My attention snapped back to that man. His clear blue eyes, devoid of disease, stared into mine. His mouth kept moving, but the sounds that came from him were less agitated. Softer. Soothing.

He reached out a hand and took mine. He lifted my hand in his, forcing my attention downward to my hand.

Finally, he gently pulled me forward.

I did not move.

He pulled again, gently. Soothing sounds were still coming from his mouth. With those sounds, he was trying to tell me something.

I stepped forward. One step.

The man's mouth lifted at the corners. It was a nice shift of his face. He gently tugged my hand as he stepped backward.

I looked down at my hand in his. How odd it was to be holding a human hand.

I stepped forward. One more step. Then he took a step. I took another step.

I stood in front of the open box. Still holding my hand, the man stood to the side, pointing into the box.

I knew what he wanted. More of that strange sense of fear rushed through me. I looked at the man again. The corners of his mouth lifted upward higher.

Behind me, I heard the second man making more angry sounds. I looked over my shoulder at him. He still had the gun pointed at my head. Beyond him, other humans were gathering. Staring. All of them making strange noises. Excited. Scared. Maybe curious. But mostly scared.

The first man tugged my hand gently.

He stepped onto the wooden block. With my hand still in his, he backed into the metal box.

Excited and angry noises coming from the gathered humans filled my head. They were even more scared. But not for themselves. They were scared for the man who was leading me into the box.

Curiosity made me look at him. Still making those soothing sounds at me, he nodded and waved me into the box with him.

I let his hand drop.

Silence filled the surrounding area.

The grass crunched underneath the feet of the man with the gun. He was stepping closer to me. Preparing to kill me.

I looked down and stepped onto the wooden block. Putting my hands flat on the floor of the metal box, I pushed my body into the opening.

As soon as my feet cleared the opening, the door slammed shut behind me.

I was trapped. With the first man.

CHAPTER
THREE

WITH THE BOX SHUT, I settled into stillness. I could see clearly in the dark. On the far end of the box, the man squatted with his back to the corner. His eyes were wide with fear. He had his hands raised up before him as though he were expecting an attack.

I stayed still. The only sound in the box was of him breathing heavily. After a moment, I could hear his heart pounding. I could smell the adrenaline caused by his fear.

I waited and watched him.

After a while, his face contorted. His smell shifted. Fear mingled with pain. Slowly, as silently as he could, he lowered his hands to the side and braced them against the sides of the box. He moved one leg forward, then the other, and scooted downward until he was sitting, his legs in front of him.

If I reached out, I could have touched his feet. The box wasn't that big.

Still, I stayed motionless.

Sudden banging from outside the box, accompanied with loud voices, made the man jump.

I cocked my head, still watching him.

He turned his head toward the sounds and shouted back some response. The noises from outside stopped.

He sat staring in my direction. Suddenly, I realized the man could not see me. He simply sat in the quiet for a while. While he sat, his breathing calmed, his heartbeat slowed, and the smell of fear slowly disappeared.

He started making sounds with his mouth. As he did, he reached a hand down along the side of his body into a pocket. He pulled something out and played with it.

Suddenly, a spark flashed. A small flame appeared. He had a lighter and by its light, he could see me.

He jumped a little at seeing me, but then the sides of his mouth shifted upward again.

Making more sounds at me, he patted his body with his free hand. He did it again and made a sound. Then he repeated it. Several times.

He pointed at me, at his mouth, and at me again.

I opened my mouth and tried to imitate the sounds he was making.

He tapped his body and said the sound, then pointed at me.

I tried to make the sound.

"Mmmm. Aye. Khllllll."

The man nodded; the strange shape of his mouth even wider. He smelled of excitement. No more fear at all.

He said the sound as he motioned for me to try.

"Michael."

The mashing of sounds passing through my lips sounded strange to my ears. It felt strange to my tongue. And yet, it also felt like a faded memory.

The man clapped one of his hands against his leg excitedly. He bobbed his head up and down. That lift to his mouth was somehow welcoming.

I tried to say the sound once more. "Michael. Michael. Michael."

Keeping my attention on the man, who I figured out called himself Michael, I moved to the opposite corner of the box. I copied the way he was sitting. Legs out in front of me, I leaned my body back against the sides of the box.

Staring at him, I tried to make my mouth copy the shape his made.

I watched his face. That contortion on his face slowly faded away as he watched me. He leaned forward, watching me in the dim light of his little flame. He waved at me with his other hand and nodded. Something in his eyes encouraged me to keep trying.

Michael made another sound, then pointed at that contortion on his face as he said it. He pointed at me, and I tried to copy the face.

I tried to copy the sound.

"Ssssmmmmaaiill."

He shook his head, repeated the sound, and pointed at me.

I copied his face. I could feel the corners of my mouth shifting upward. The strange contortion made my eyes squint a little. I stopped and tried anew. Then I twisted my face and tried the sound once more.

"Smile."

Michael made the contorted face once more, this time letting out a series of coughing sounds, but not of illness. I breathed in. The strange sounds matched the smell.

It was a smell of contentment. The sounds were of something opposite of fear and rage. A sensation passed over my body, a strange warmth from my inside. Tearing my gaze away from the man, I touched my body. I pressed my hands to my chest, where the warmth felt most intense. My hands felt no such warmth. Just the tattered remnants of clothing I died and was reborn in. Just the grotesque body reanimated by disease and rage.

I liked the warmth, but it was new. It was also scary. The man continued to stare at me intently. I tried to match his smile. I think I did it right, because he smiled right back. In that instant, I knew a smile was a good thing. It was a thing from a life I'd lost long ago, but maybe I could have it once more.

Another new yet strangely familiar feeling washed over me to match the warmth in my chest.

Hope. Its flicker in my mind confused me.

———

Pounding on the box caused Michael to fall quiet. The man pointed at me, then at himself. He gestured to the end of the box I was leaning on, to me next, and finally to the corner where he was sitting. He shifted to a crouch, all the while continuing his gesturing.

The sounds he made were too fast for me to make sense of. But I figured out what his pointing meant. He wanted to switch spots with me.

There was more pounding on the walls of the box. He turned his head toward the sound and made his own shouted sounds in response. The pounding stopped, and the humans outside the box responded with vocalizations.

Michael looked back at me and made that same pointing motion. I imitated him and moved my body so it was low but balanced on my two feet. He shuffled toward me while he motioned for me to shuffle around him. After some moving around, I was crouched in his corner, and he was knocking on the end of the box where I had just been.

The end of the box opened. Bright light spilled in. Hands reached inside and pulled Michael out.

Then the opening closed, and I was in darkness once again. This time alone.

Sitting in the box's darkness did not bother me. I remained sitting and simply listened to the humans outside. Voices rose, fell, and grew distant. Through tiny pinprick holes throughout the box, daylight passed into night, and night into day. Through the thin metal walls of my cage, the sounds of movement around the camp ebbed and flowed, but no one returned to open the box. So, I stayed stationary.

Another day passed. Another night. As dim light filtered into the box after that night, the rumble of engines started.

A strange feeling rushed through me. Getting to my feet, I found a tiny hole and tried to peer through it. Limited to just a tiny view directly in front of the box, I saw the humans had torn down their camp. They were getting ready to move. I strained to see if I could find the Michael human, but finally gave up as the sun passed overhead and the light in the box shifted.

A sudden lurch of the box and I ended up sprawled in a jumbled heap on the floor. Lying there, trying to understand what was happening, I realized the box was moving. The humans were taking me with them, wherever it was they were going next. I continued to lie there without moving, just getting used to the feel of movement under me. The box bounced and shifted from side to side, tossing my body up and down.

The box kept moving until the light of day shifted into the dark of night and everything stopped. Engines quieted. Humans' voices called out a few brief things I didn't understand, and after that, all was quiet once more.

I stood up and moved to the hole I had stared out of before. The darkness beyond the box was impenetrable, but somewhere to the side I could just make out the vague flickering of what must have been a campfire. I stood back from the wall, moved to the left, and tried to find another hole I could look out of. When I didn't find one, I sat back down and leaned against the wall farthest from the door.

And I waited.

Light filtered into the box once more. Engines roared to life. The box shuddered forward. Before it had moved, though, someone had pounded on the box. A voice yelled, and it took me a moment to realize it was Michael. He pounded and yelled some more, so I pounded back and tried to say his name.

I tried to say it but could not seem to form the sounds. Instead, whatever came out of my mouth sounded like any other zombie sound I had made before. So, I simply pounded back.

Beyond that, nothing new happened, so I remained seated and when the box moved again, I shifted down onto the floor, so I was lying on my back. Like the day before, I stared upward, just watching the light shift and change from morning to afternoon to evening.

When the light turned orange, I realized it was nearing nighttime. I expected the box to lurch to a stop, but it did not. Instead, it kept moving for a long while into the dark hours of the night before it finally jerked to a stop.

A strange smell permeated the metal box. I sniffed it. I tasted the air with my mangled tongue. Humans. A lot of them. So many, I could smell their adrenaline, their sweat, the odors of their waste, the odors of their fears and their joys. We had come to a settlement.

Sudden hunger nearly overwhelmed me. I stood up and peered through the hole again, trying to view my surroundings. Although it was night, bright lights shone atop a high wall, lighting up the area in front of it. The humans from the camp were staring upward. One of them yelled something to someone on the wall. This went on for a while. Then I saw the silhouette of a man step forward. He waved an arm in my direction as he shouted up at the human on the wall. That went on for a while too, but none of it held any meaning to me.

After a while, the man on the ground turned toward the box. He called out to some others and came walking toward the box. I stepped away from the tiny hole and turned to stare toward the door. Sure enough, it opened. Several bright lights shone into the box, blinding me. I stood still, listening and waiting.

A man was making sounds with his mouth. He stepped into the light where I could see and hear him better. It was Michael. He waved his arms at me. He wanted me to walk toward him. I moved slowly. Soon, I was at the edge of the box, looking down at the ground.

Without warning, two other men reached out and grabbed me, pulling me to the ground. Another draped something over my head and tightened it around my neck, cutting off my vision. Something pulled my arms forward and bound them to each other.

Voices continued to ring out. They were excited, but also scared. Among them, I heard the man with whom I was most familiar. Michael's voice was much calmer, almost soothing. There was something about it, like a pleading note. The humans pulled me to my feet. I heard two of them behind me, one pushing me ahead of them.

As I moved forward, I heard humans moving all around me. The stink of fear flooded me. I paused, but was shoved from behind, and nearly fell over. As I walked, the ground under my feet felt hard. Unyielding. Not the softness of dirt and grass, but the hardness of something manufactured. It tore at the bottoms of my feet, though it did not hurt. The humans pushed me onward. And onward. Strange sounds filled my ears. Hushed voices. Loud voices. Wood smacking against wood. Metal clicking. Metallic squealing and screeching.

The ground changed from stonelike to cold metallic, like the box. Someone shoved me forward roughly. As I fell to the ground, the covering over my head was yanked off.

I hit the metallic floor hard, rolled onto my back, and stared at the humans that had brought me to this place. One pulled an open metal wall across the opening. I heard metal hitting metal and the clicking sound of something closing. Staring through the metal bars, I saw Michael talk animatedly to a man in a white coat and another man in a dirty leather jacket.

After the excited exchange, he walked toward me. His face stretched into a smile, but it was not the same smile he'd shown in the box. It was different. It was forced. Fearful. I stared up at him from where I lay. He stepped up to the bars and leaned on them with his hands.

Michael motioned for me to get up. I did. Why not?

He pointed to my face.

"Smile," he said. He showed me his, and he pointed to me.

I understood.

I carefully worked to lift the corners of my mouth to imitate the shape of his mouth.

He nodded and glanced at the two men behind him, who were watching us.

Next, he looked back at me and said, "Smile."

He waved a hand at me, pointed to his mouth as he repeated, "Smile."

I understood.

I worked hard to form my mouth the right way.

"Sssmmaaiill."

His mouth shifted into the same smile he had shown me in the box. He glanced over his shoulder. I followed his gaze, my face frozen in my imitation of his smile. The looks on the faces of the other men with their eyes wide, their mouths gaping, touched something in me.

A strange hiccup left my mouth. Michael's head swiveled to look at me. His own eyes were wide.

Sounds erupted from his mouth, but I didn't understand them. Still, I wondered if I had surprised him.

CHAPTER FOUR

THE HUMANS DID NOT REMAIN LONG. After they left, I sat in the center of the cell. Time passed and soon enough, it was the next day. Lights came on illuminating the cell and the area before it. A door opened, and a new man stepped in with Michael at his side.

The man wore white over his clothing. He stared at me while Michael approached the bars and made noises at me. Some noises were becoming recognizable. He'd said them before, always when first approaching me. I tried to emulate the first one he said.

"Hhhhh. Elllll. Ooooh."

His mouth lifted into that wide thing he called a smile. He looked at the other man, a flurry of sounds filling the room. The man in white simply nodded and kept watching.

Michael's smile dropped from his face, but he turned back to face me. He made a motion with his hands, indicating he wanted me to come closer.

I watched him for a moment. He had a small cylinder in one hand with something thin and long on the end. Not knowing what the thing was, I glanced back up at the man. He lifted his mouth and smiled at me again, still waving me over while repeating the same sound over and over.

"Come closer," he said.

I got to my feet and shuffled to the bars. Still staring at him, I copied the sounds.

"Cooome clllooosss uurrr."

The sounds felt strange in my ears. But the effect they had on him was instant.

He still stared at me, then he lifted the little cylinder to show me. He pointed at my hand, then he put out one of his. I raised my hand and held it out to him in the same way. With his hand, he reached through the bars and took my hand, holding it at the wrist. He laid the cylinder along the top of it. Then he pressed the point of the cylinder until the thin part slipped into my skin. I watched him. I felt nothing. He was watching the cylinder, so I watched it as well.

The end of the cylinder was filling with thick, black fluid.

My blood.

When the end of the cylinder was full, he pulled it away and back through the bars. He turned away from me and gave the cylinder to the man in white.

That man still stared at me. His expression was one of shock and fear, but also something else. Something like what I saw increasingly on the Michael's face. The man in white tucked the cylinder into a pocket before he turned and left.

Michael watched the door close before he turned back toward me. He sat on the floor by the bars and motioned for me to do the same.

I did. Somehow, I knew he'd spend the day with me. Somehow, I knew he was there to help me learn more sounds.

Throughout the day, other humans came and went. They stood watching me interact with the Michael, who appeared delighted when I said his name. Throughout the day, Michael and I practiced more words. They brought him food and drink. I could tell they were considering what I might want to eat, but ended up ignoring the question.

For some, the ones carrying the weapons; I moved away from the bars. For others, particularly the two younger ones, I stepped closer, wanting to get better looks at them. Young humans were incredibly rare. Most didn't survive the initial spread of the pathogen that started the apocalypse. Few humans found the ability to reproduce while being on the run.

Most of the time, however, it was just me and Michael.

The day wore on, and I got better at mimicking the sounds. I even understood some and started making connections between others.

The light outside grew dim. Michael glanced up. He got to his feet.

He pointed to himself first, then to the door next as he spoke slowly, "It is late. I must go."

I wasn't sure of the exact meaning, but I got the gist. He was going to leave me.

I remained seated and made no sounds. He said an unfamiliar word and motioned for me to say it as well.

"Ghhhhooood. Bbbbiiiii."

He smiled and left.

―――

The days passed from light to dark to light again. Several in succession until I lost track of time.

Michael came to see me every day. He spent most days entirely with me, helping me learn how to talk.

Occasionally, the man in the white coat would come with him. He'd sit on a chair with a thing called a notebook and do something called writing.

I understood he was writing about me. Of course, I knew I was changing, but I didn't know why that mattered, nor why that was interesting to Michael and the man in white.

Sometimes, other people would come in as well. At one point, another man in a white coat came in and indicated he needed to take another cylinder of my blood. With Michael keeping watch, I held out my arm and watched them take another full sample of my blood.

Other times, people who were simply curious would come and sit by the wall behind Michael and just watch us as we made sounds.

Finally, one morning, Michael came in with two armed men beside him. The men appeared cautious and smelled of fear and anxiety. But Michael smelled calm and excited.

He motioned to the door.

"Today, we are going outside," he said.

I glanced at the small window at the back of my cell before looking at Michael, a smile, something I was doing more in his company, shifting my mouth.

"Outside," I repeated.

Michael nodded and pointed to the two men.

"They are coming with us because people are afraid. But you and I are going to show them you are different. They do not need to fear you."

"Fear me," I repeated. The concepts of feelings expressed in words were hard for me to grasp. But the smell coming off the men matched what I thought Michael meant.

I pointed at the men. "Men afraid."

Both men glared at me. One whispered to Michael. His face grew dark, and he responded to them in a tone that caught my attention. It caught theirs as well. They immediately nodded at him and avoided looking at me.

Michael opened the metal bars and motioned me to join him on the other side.

Together, we stepped toward a door that I had not seen used before. He opened it, and the room was flooded with sunlight. Michael stepped outside and held the door for me.

I followed him, aware of the two men stepping out behind me.

I looked around. With the building at my back, I realized I was inside a large human compound. Immediately in front of me was a large grassy area. A few small trees were scattered about, and beyond them stood a row of buildings. These were newly built concrete structures. Each window had bars over them. Each door looked like it was made from solid steel. They were zombie proof.

To the left, I saw more trees and a tall wall beyond them. To the right, patches of earth were split into rows. The humans were going to grow new food.

Besides Michael and the two men behind me, I didn't see any other humans.

Michael said, "Come. Let us walk."

"Walk," I repeated and fell into step beside him as he led the way toward the trees.

As we walked, Michael pointed to things, giving me human words for objects I was familiar with.

I copied him, saying the sounds for tree, grass, flower, sky.

When we were among the trees, I learned the words leaf, trunk, branch, and soil.

A sound filtered down from the trees. I looked up and raised my hand at it.

Michael looked up and saw what I was pointing at.

He smiled and said, "That is a bird."

"Bird," I repeated.

I watched the bird as it hopped from branch to branch, making little chirps and whistles.

I tried to copy the sounds.

Michael laughed. He turned me to face him.

"No. No. Try this." He motioned to his face. He puckered his lips, emphasizing the formation of his mouth with his hands. Then he blew air out and a sound similar to the bird's escaped.

I stared at him. He repeated the shape of his lips and the exhalation of air; he pointed at me.

"Now, you try."

I felt my lips. They were not plump and healthy like his. But with my fingers on them, I felt them shift into what I hoped was the right formation. But no sound came through. I tried but still made no sound.

Michael watched. Then he stopped me. He lifted one of my hands to his mouth and made the sound again. I felt warm air move out of his mouth.

I dropped my hand to my side and tried to make the bird sound another time.

One guard said something behind me. I didn't catch it, so I turned to him. Michael did the same.

"Say that again," he said to the guard.

"Zombies don't breathe."

"Breathe," I repeated.

Frowning, Michael looked at me, disappointed.

He motioned me away from the tree with the bird in it. We moved on, and he continued to point at things and help me say what they were.

When the light was growing dim, he led me back to the cell. Once I was secured behind the bars, the guards left. Michael remained standing; his expression was new to me.

"This is my last day with you. The doctor and his team want to study you. Tomorrow, you will be moved to their research facility." He paused. Once again, I understood only bits and pieces. I knew the doctor. I understood moved. I didn't understand *study* or *research* or *facility*.

Michael continued, "Before you go, I want you to have a name. Names have a way of humanizing things for other humans. I want to make sure they remember you were once human, and whatever you are now, you are something special."

All the sounds he made ran together, but I understood name.

"Name," I said.

Michael bobbed his head up and down and pointed at me as he said, "Name."

I touched my chest and repeated, "Name."

After a few minutes of silence, Michael pointed at me, "Adam."

I repeated, "Aahhh daaaammm."

Michael smiled, "Yes. Adam. You are Adam. Fitting, because you are the first of a new thing. So, now you are Adam."

He pointed at me, and said it again, "Adam. You are Adam."

I pointed at myself, "I... am... Adam."

Michael's face lit up. The aroma coming from him was one of joy and hope.

Then he grew serious.

"Goodbye, Adam," he said and walked away before I could answer.

To the space where he'd been standing, I said, "Goodbye."

I turned and looked out the high window.

I said into the silence, "I am Adam."

CHAPTER **FIVE**

MICHAEL WAS RIGHT.

The man in the white coat came for me with several other men dressed in loose fitting blue outfits. The ones in blue bound my wrists together, inserted a bit between my teeth, and forced me out of the cell and out of the building. They had me climb into another metal box on the back of a vehicle and locked me inside. We didn't travel far before they stopped the vehicle and had me get out of the box.

Looking around, I noticed we were behind a larger building on the far side of the human settlement. This structure was more impressive than others. It had thicker walls and stood much taller, with small windows high on the upper stories. Barbed wire ran around the outside, and a concrete trench wrapped around it. A retracting metal plate covering the trench allowed us to walk across and into the building.

The men led me down several long halls and up a series of steps until we reached a small room completely encased with glass. They pushed me inside. As I stood there, I stared through the glass on one side of the room, observing men and women in white coats working over various machines. They wore masks that covered their faces entirely, and heavy blue gloves. Their coats protected them from neck to floor, and their feet were wrapped in some sort of blue covering.

I turned to look through the glass on the other side of the glass room. In the next room were a desk, a chair, and several screens that showed views of other rooms.

The door slid shut behind me. I glanced at the man in the white coat. He hadn't tried to talk to me. He just stared at me.

I ignored him and looked about my new cage. Opposite the door I'd come in was another door that led into a long room with a series of empty metal tables. Each one had heavy leather straps screwed to them. I knew what they were for. And I knew why I was brought there.

I was to be studied.

I turned my attention back to the screens.

Although it was hard to tell from where I stood, it appeared as if the screens were looking into cells like mine. I stepped toward the glass wall and leaned forward until my head rested against the wall.

Ignoring the man in the coat as he entered that room and sat at the desk, I peered at the screens. I was only vaguely aware that the man picked up a small black device and pointed it at one screen.

The image changed to show an overview of the cell I was in. I saw myself watching the screen.

The man, who was still staring at me, stood in silence.

I pointed at the screen.

"Adam," I said. Then I pointed at me and repeated it.

The man did not respond. Instead, he turned to the screens and pointed the black device at them. One by one, the screens changed, showing better views of the rooms I'd seen before.

Each room held a zombie. Most were stationary. Some were pacing the cells aimlessly.

Why was he showing me the others they had captured?

I looked back at the man. His face was blank, and he didn't talk to me as Michael had. He simply stared. He pointed the black device in my direction. The glass between us slowly turned from see-through, to opaque, to silvery, until I could no longer see him on the other side. Instead, I was staring at my reflection.

Initially, I had no interest in my reflection.

I turned my back on it and realized all the glass surrounding me reflected myself at me. I could no longer see beyond my cell.

I stepped to the middle of the room, sat on the floor, and waited.

Soon, a door opened behind me, the one opposite the door I had entered. Twisting to see through the open door, I watched two people enter. They were covered from head to toe in more of the blue clothing and equipment that hid their faces from me. I could not tell if these were people I had been around before.

One approached me cautiously.

"I was told you can speak," said the human.

Its voice passed through a filtered mask, so I could not determine whether the human was a man or a woman.

"I speak," I said back.

The masked faces looked at each other, the second human muttering under its breath, "No shit."

The first one looked back at me and said, "We need you to come with us."

I stayed sitting.

The human pointed to the door they had come in through. "There are tests we need to do, and we need to do them in that room."

I stared through the door at the metal tables with restraints.

"Tests," I repeated.

"Yes. Tests. Come with us."

The second person stepped toward me and placed a hand on my shoulder. Just a hand resting on my shoulder, but I knew it was intended as the beginning of a threat.

I got to my feet slowly and looked all about the cell, but there was nothing to see. Only the reflections of the three of us. The first person stepped toward the door and waited for me to follow.

The second person moved to stand behind me.

I walked to the door and investigated the room. Without waiting to be told, I walked to the closest table and lay down on it.

Both humans rushed toward me and quickly strapped me to the table. I heard them both mumbling things under their breath: *scary, what the heck is going on, what kind of zombie is this? I have to get out of here.*

I stayed perfectly still while they worked the straps onto my wrists and ankles, across my neck, and a final one across the top of my head.

I couldn't smell their fear through their suits, but I heard it in their muttered comments.

"Not afraid," I said to them as I tapped my chest.

They both jerked upright and stepped away from me.

The second one said, "You should be."

They closed the door to my cell and left the room through another door.

Only silence remained.

―――――

I didn't know how long I remained on that table, but I estimated it was almost a dozen days.

Humans in blue came in, poked me with things they called needles, and left. They rolled in machines that buzzed and whirred. They placed black plates under me, beside me, moving up and down my body, from one side to another. That procedure they did many times. It was a lengthy process. So lengthy that sometimes, midway, the humans would swap out.

One test they did, they rolled in a machine that completely encompassed the table I was on. When they ran it, the light inside the machine spun all about me, making me confused and disoriented. They used that machine a few times as well, focusing on my head.

None of the humans bothered talking to me. They only talked to each other. So, I listened and continued to learn.

At first, they only talked about the tests that were to be done on me. The needles that pulled fluid from me were to test my blood. One test where they poked at my back tested something they called spinal fluid. Another test, using a long needle, they used to test the air in my lungs. On and on.

They had considered doing a test called a colonoscopy on me, but another test, something they called an x-ray, showed that I no longer had any organs in my lower body that resembled those of the human body. I didn't understand what that meant, but after a while, they shifted their tests to my head, specifically my brain.

The big whirling machine with the silly lights was looking at my brain. The humans had questions about what my brain looked like, and they talked a lot about the results from that test. They talked a lot about the results from the blood tests, too. Something about a DNA test. And a genome test. All words I was unfamiliar with, but words they repeated a great deal the first several days I was on that table.

But after those first days, the conversations shifted. The humans talked about other things. Words I was beginning to understand became the focal point of their conversations as they worked on me. Family. Spouses. Children. Life. Then a conversation that speculated having to leave the settlement. Having to move on to a new life. Each time that conversation came up, I could sense their hesitation and fear.

This was not something I understood, but the longer I lay on that table, the more I shared the concerns the people were voicing.

Through it all, none of them ever spoke to me. They did not ask me questions. They did not address me. None of them called me by my new name. I didn't see Michael again.

But one day, that changed. The man in the white coat came into the room. He did not wear all the strange clothing. No mask. No gloves.

He stood over me for a moment, just staring down at me.

Then he pulled a small metal chair over and sat beside me.

I had to twist my head in a funny way to see him, but I stared back.

We sat like that. Just staring at each other.

Finally, he spoke.

"They call you Adam," he said.

His voice was smooth, calm, low. He stared into my eyes as though he were trying to see something in them.

I said nothing. I just stared back at him, waiting for him to continue.

He said nothing for a while. Then he stood up and, looking down at me, he asked, "Do you understand questions? Can you answer questions?"

I stared up at him.

"If you would like to sit up, or walk around, say 'yes'."

Unable to move my head even a little, but not feeling a powerful urge to move, I continued to stare at the man. His mouth turned downward, opposite the smiles that lit up Michael's face during our interactions. Michael called the downward turn a frown.

I said, "Frown."

The man's frown deepened, but then he reached across me and undid the latch for the restraint that held that wrist. Quickly, he undid the other hand. He moved to my ankles and removed the straps from them as well. He moved back up to my head.

"I hope you won't make me regret this, Adam," he said.

Next, he undid the strap that crossed my neck and the one that crossed my head.

He stepped away from the table and stood behind the chair, watching me.

I kept staring back at him as I shifted my body into a sitting position with my legs and feet dangling over the side of the table.

The man ran his gaze over my body. He asked, "Do you feel any pain? Or are you cold?"

"No pain," I said. The words were hoarse and dry in my mouth. I had to work my tongue loose from the roof of my mouth to even begin to say 'no.'

The man nodded and asked, "Is it okay that I sit here with you?"

He pointed at the chair as he asked.

"Chair," I said back to him, and watched him move around the metal object and sit down. Once he was seated, he leaned back and crossed his arms.

"Adam, I'm Doctor Cal Odensea."

I repeated, "Dooktur Kaaallodenseee."

A flicker of a smile touched the man's face.

"Close enough," he said. "Do you know why you are here?"

I stared at him while I tried to make sense of his question. After a moment, I said, "Fear."

He frowned and did not respond immediately, as though he were thinking about my response. Finally, he nodded and said, "Yes. Fear. If you mean we fear you, sadly, you would be right. I hope you can understand what I'm about to tell you, because from this point on, I need your help to find answers to some scary questions."

He paused, but I said nothing. He took a deep breath, and continued, "You are a new thing, Adam. Entirely new. From the beginning of the outbreak, we have been trying to find a way to stop and cure the virus that kills us and reanimates us into zombies. We have had no luck. For over a decade, I have been traveling from settlement to settlement trying to find a solution. I was about to give up, but then

Michael brought you here. You change everything. Do you understand?"

I said nothing.

He leaned forward and flipped my wrist over. He tapped a vein that sat under my skin. Tapping it, he said, "Your heart does not beat. Nor do you breathe. Still, your brain is healing itself, and your body is appearing to heal. But both things defy science as we have known it. The zombies defy logic and science. That is why we can't stop the change, and why we can't cure it. But you..."

He paused and leaned back in his chair as he looked me in the eye once more.

"You, Adam, make the zombie virus look tame. The changes happening to you break all the rules of medical science. You are a walking point of terror for humanity, because we don't know what this means for us. We don't know what this means for zombies. And so, I need to do more testing on you. I need to get to know you. I need to study both your strange blood and your healing brain. Because I believe you are sentient, I need to ask you to help me."

I stared at him. I understood most of what he was saying. I didn't understand the complexities, of course, but I understood he wanted my help. I understood he wanted me to give him help as my own choice. The concept was foreign to me, yet welcome and strangely satisfying.

Imitating his head movement, I nodded.

"I will help," I said.

CHAPTER SIX

THE MAN LEFT NOT long after I said I would help with additional testing.

He left me unbound and did not return me to the cell I had been in. I stayed on the table and looked around. Two other metal tables sat in the room. Under each of the tables, the floor sloped down to a hole with a metal grate on top.

As I sat in the empty room, I listened to the sounds from nearby machinery mixing with the buzz of human voices. It sounded as though there was a grouping of people nearby, so I got up and moved toward the buzz. Sure enough, as I got near the wall at the far end of the room, I could hear the voices more clearly, though the people were talking so fast I couldn't make out words.

One voice was the low, soft tones of the man in the white coat. The other was the familiar voice of Michael. There were two other voices I was not familiar with. They were not the voices of the others who had done test after test on me.

Unable to understand what they were saying, I moved back to the table and sat down.

After a while, the far door opened and the man in the white coat came in.

"Doctor Cal Odensea," I said more carefully and more clearly as he approached.

Behind him, Michael stepped into the room. I quickly created the smile we greeted each other with during our time together. He smiled back and stood beside the man in the white coat.

"I have asked Michael to help us as we continue these next phases of testing. You've learned a great deal from him, and he has agreed to keep teaching you language and what things mean."

I stared at the man for a moment, before shifting my gaze to Michael.

"Friend. Michael," I said.

Michael bobbed his head up and down, his smile wide.

"Yes, Adam. I am your friend. And Doctor Cal Odensea is your doctor. Do you understand what doctor means?"

I stared in silence. Michael glanced at the other man.

"A doctor is a person who tries to help people. Some doctors try to heal people. Other doctors try to heal people's minds. And some doctors like Dr. Odensea study and learn how things work in the human body to help prevent illness and death. Do you understand?"

I said, "Tests."

Michael nodded. "Yes. He will do a lot of tests to understand you better."

He stepped toward me. His face grew dark, and he stared at me with concern. In a low voice, he asked, "Have the people here hurt you, Adam?"

"Hurt," I repeated.

Michael paused, then said, "Remember when I taught you how to answer yes or no to some questions? I need you to tell me yes or no, now. Have the people doing the tests on you hurt you?"

I didn't understand. So, I stayed silent.

Michael turned to Dr. Odensea. "Does he show any reaction to pain?"

The doctor shook his head.

Michael stepped closer to me. He said, "When someone hits me, it causes me pain. It hurts. When I have those needles put in my arms, the needles cause me pain. It hurts. Do you understand?"

I said, "Yes."

"Very good. Okay. When they put needles in your arms, did that cause you pain? Hurt?"

"No," I said. "No pain. No hurt."

Michael stepped back and leaned against another table. He gave a small smile.

"That is very good, Adam. I am glad that you are not being hurt," he said.

Dr. Odensea gave Michael a dark look, then he turned to me and said, "Tomorrow, Michael will come in and teach you more. As you two work together, I will conduct more tests on your brain." He paused in thought before he asked, "Adam, we've given you no food or water. Do you need to eat?"

I understood what he was asking, but the idea of attacking and eating made me uneasy. I looked at Michael, "Food. Yes. Not human."

Dr. Odensea looked at Michael, who shrugged in response as he said, "When he was in the other cell, I brought him rabbits and rats. He seemed to like them well enough, but he didn't need to eat like we do. He only ate twice."

Dr. Odensea said, "Well, we've not given it anything at all since it's been with us. It was a point of some concern. Some others thought we should give it a cadaver, others thought we should give it some blood, and one even thought we should just give it some brains. Something they saw on an old zombie show or movie. So, we never really decided what to do."

"So, you've been letting *him* starve," said Michael, his voice heavy and with a strange emphasis on *him*.

The doctor shrugged. "I will see it is brought a rabbit right away. In the meantime, please see it to its cell?"

Without waiting for a response, he turned and left the room.

I got to my feet and moved toward the door to my cell. Michael joined me at the door and placed his hand on a metal pad to one side. The door slid open, revealing the mirrored space within. I hesitated. I was beginning to dislike seeing myself from every angle.

Michael looked inside. He muttered something under his breath, but I couldn't make out the words. He turned to a small set of buttons next to the metal pad, and tapping several of them, he transformed the room. Instead of mirrors reflecting my image back to me, or the translucent glass allowing me to see beyond the room, one wall was a floor to ceiling view of the outside. Grass. Trees. Clouds rolling through the skies. All the other walls were a dirt color. Not harsh but calming.

"Friend," I said to Michael and stepped into the room.

He stood in the doorway while I sat on the floor in the center of the room and stared at the picture of the world I missed.

"I think you meant *thank you*. You are welcome, Adam."

He shut the door, and I was left in silence.

Time passed with the doctor and Michael visiting every day. Michael to teach me. The doctor to observe me. Before each session with Michael, the doctor, and some others who he referred to as his research staff, would apply little metal objects that were connected to wires, to my head. They would connect those wires to a machine that sat beside me. On the other side of the machine, the doctor sat watching a screen that showed an image of my brain. On some rare occasions, he'd get excited about something on the screen and would turn it around to show Michael. Of course, I could see it too, but I didn't understand what I was seeing, nor what about the changes in light on the screen meant, or why the doctor cared so much about all of it.

The more I learned, and the more testing he conducted, the more enthusiastic the doctor became. After an afternoon of something called word association, where Michael showed me a series of pictures and asked me to tell him what I thought they were images of, the doctor stopped the session abruptly.

"Michael, that is enough for today. I have so much data here, it will take me days to sort through it all."

Michael sat back in his chair, watching me for a moment, then he looked at Dr. Odensea, "Then let's take off the nodes and just allow Adam to learn at a more relaxed pace."

The doctor was still staring at the screen, a strange expression of almost wonder on his face. He pointed to the screen with one hand while he turned it toward us with the other.

He said, "Adam's brain is reconstructing itself. And since we've begun the more intensive sessions, its brain is rebuilding at an even greater rate!" He stopped and looked at me, then at Michael.

"The implications..." he said in a low voice. He looked back at me, wonder plain in his eyes as he said, "The implications... Adam, you could very well become even more intelligent and advanced than humanity."

I heard Michael inhale sharply, but I held the doctor's stare. I asked, "What does that mean?"

He looked back at the screen and tapped at his chin with the end of his pencil.

After a moment, he said, "It means that you are a walking scientific miracle. Biologically, you make no sense. You do not eat or drink or breathe like a human or a zombie. You are smarter than a zombie for sure, and you have the capabilities of being smarter than the smartest human. You could very well be the next step in the evolution of humanity."

"But I am not human, you said."

The doctor lowered the pencil to the portable table that held the screen. Twisting in his chair, a look of confusion on his face, he answered, "You are not human. The virus that turned you into a zombie completely changed your genetic make-up. You share genes with our kind, but like other zombies, you lost a piece of the sequence."

He looked at Michael, explaining more to him than to me, because he knew I did not yet understand the things he talked about when he spoke of genetics. I simply knew it to mean what I was made of, though he insisted it was much more elaborate than that.

To Michael, he continued, "I finally got the most recent results of the genetic testing we did on Adam. Its genome is changing. Actively. It is not human. It is not really a zombie. Not anymore."

I glanced at Michael, who said nothing. He absorbed the doctor's statement.

After a few minutes, Michael said, "I don't guess it matters. Does it? We still don't know why. Why is Adam changing?"

Dr. Odensea sat back in his chair.

He ran a hand through his thinning hair, exhaled loudly, and rubbed his face as though exhausted.

"Well, I have a hypothesis, but I haven't done the testing yet," he said.

"Hypothesis?" I asked.

Michael responded, "A hypothesis is an educated guess about the potential solution to a problem. In this case, the problem is that we do not know why you are changing as you are." He looked at the doctor and asked, "So, what is your hypothesis?"

Dr. Odensea said, "I think Adam was infected by a new virus. Or the zombie virus itself is mutating. Of course, Adam is the only one we have seen this in, so that may not be it at all, but..."

I interrupted, "I met another like me."

Both Michael and the doctor snapped their heads to look at me.

Michael demanded, "Repeat that?"

I said, "Before I came to your camp, Michael. I was with a horde. Just wandering with them. I already knew I was different. Changing. The horde knew it, or sensed it, too. But one day, while I was wandering aimlessly with them, I met another. But it moved on, and I was..."

I paused as I thought of what the right word was to express what I meant. "I feared it. Or it feared me? I don't know how to describe it. But it was as though we were like those magnets you were teaching me about. We just couldn't be around each other."

The doctor was scribbling furiously on his pad. After he stopped, he looked up at me.

"Do you remember anything about that one?" he asked. "Do you think you could find it if you could leave here?"

I looked at Michael, whose face was curiously blank.

"I don't know," I answered honestly. "I don't know that I would want to find it. All I recall is that I knew it was like me because of the way we looked at each other. There was a lack of rage in its eyes. But that is all I recall."

Dr. Odensea set his pad and pencil down and leaned back with a sigh. "Oh well. It would have been nice to have two of you to do this research with. Compare notes on your learning abilities. See if its brain is repairing like yours. If its body continues to function as yours does, in a way that makes no biological sense."

He got up and looked at Michael.

"You are welcome to remain as long as you wish. Adam doesn't appear to need to sleep as we do. Some of the staff think it is almost a version of a vampire the way it goes on and on, with no apparent need for rest."

He laughed.

As he walked away from us, I heard him mutter under his breath, "A zombie vampire. That would be everything."

CHAPTER SEVEN

"WELL, Adam, how are you doing today," Dr. Odensea asked as he entered the room.

I still lived in the glass-walled cell, but over time, Michael introduced furniture to the space. At first, just a mattress on the floor. Then a frame and a box that fit under the mattress, so the bed was up off the ground. One day, he brought in a table with two chairs.

Every time he brought in a new item, he'd ask me to try it out. He always asked me about my comfort. It was strange to him that I felt no warmth or cold, no discomfort after sitting in one position for hours at a time. It was odd to Dr. Odensea too, and so a flurry of tests was done to test something called a nervous system. I never determined if he was satisfied with the results. Michael was not. That was obvious. He made it his purpose to make me as comfortable as possible.

I shifted my focus back to Dr. Odensea as he stood in the doorway holding a small box in front of him. Michael, sitting on the chair, watched me, an amused expression on his face.

"What do you have?" I asked the doctor.

The doctor smiled and set the box on the table between Michael and me. Carefully, he lifted the lid off, revealing a food they called cake. I stared at it. It was covered in the pink and blue and white stuff they called frosting. Humans loved it. On the top of the cake, words were carefully written out: *Happy Birthday, Adam*.

I looked up at the doctor as I pointed at the cake.

"Not my birthday."

Both he and Michael laughed.

"Well," the doctor said, "we don't know when your changes started, but we know when you first came to us. You have been with us for a year."

Michael shook his head. "It's hard to believe we've been here this long..."

Then he leaned forward and ran a finger through the frosting before he stuck it in his mouth.

"Splendid stuff there, Adam. I know the lady who made it. It took her a while to get all the ingredients, so this is a real treat. You'll like it. I promise," he said after a moment.

I looked at the cake. I doubted I would like it. But it was important to Michael, it seemed, so I copied him. Running a finger through the frosting, I gathered a mix of the pink, blue, and white stuff. I held it before me, looking at it, trying to understand humans' fascination with sugary things. Feeling both men staring at me, I stuck the finger in my mouth and consumed the thick cream.

Nope.

Nothing.

Now, if it had smelled like something living and running and terrified...

I shook my head.

"Well?" prompted the doctor.

I shook my head and said, "No. Sorry."

Michael closed the box and smiled widely. "Oh well, more for me then."

He got up and left the room. The doctor didn't wait. He sat down in the chair Michael just vacated.

"As I was saying," he said, "you've been with us for a year now. I know you have trouble grasping the passing of time during the day, but you register the length of time you've been here, yes?"

I thought about it. I didn't think I registered time like humans did, but I could look around the room and see the passing of time by the number of things in the room. Each added item was a point in time. Prior to having anything in the room with me, a lot of what happened, a lot of the teaching and testing ran together so that I had a challenging time recalling which events happened first. But since adding the furniture, the books, the pictures that were taped to the glass walls, I could set events in a sort of order.

"I know that since the mattress was brought in here, time has passed, but no, I don't really grasp your concept of time," I said.

Dr. Odensea nodded as though he understood, but the look on his face told me he was a bit perplexed.

"Curious," he said.

He rose and wandered about the room. Across from the bed, Michael had set up a set of wooden shelves. Every so often, he would bring me a new book to learn to read. He told me they were children's books, but he was always so pleased when I finished one, reading it aloud, understanding different words.

Dr. Odensea lifted one of the books. It was one I had not tried yet. It was small, but its words were small and packed together. The pages were brown. No color. No pictures. Only the cover of the book was colorful. It was a picture of a rabbit standing at the edge of a field. He held the book toward me.

"You've read *Watership Down*?" he asked.

I reached out and took the book.

I said, "No. Michael wants me to, but there are no pictures. I don't think I will like it."

Dr. Odensea sat back down. He pointed at the book. "Why not read the first chapter to me, then tell me if you want to keep reading it on your own?"

I knew Dr. Odensea recorded all my sessions with Michael, but I had never read to anyone except Michael. I stared at the doctor for a minute.

"Am I being tested?" I asked.

He frowned and said, "No. Not this time. I just want to hear you read. And that book was one of my favorites when I was younger. I am interested to know if you will like it too. If you will form an opinion about it."

"Is opinion good?" I asked.

The doctor chuckled and said, "Sometimes. Sometimes not. But opinion is a step beyond reasoning. If you can form opinions, that would tell me more about how your brain works beyond its ability to learn and problem solve."

"So, this *is* a test," I said. I didn't wait for the doctor to answer. Instead, I opened the book to the first page. There was some sort of verse at the top of the page, which I ignored. Instead, I focused on the first sentence:

"The primroses were over…" and I read the first chapter.

―――

Several days after talking to Dr. Odensea about that first chapter of *Watership Down*, he had me join him in the main lab where they always did their fluid draws. They stopped calling whatever was flowing in my body blood. It carried no oxygen, no nutrients. If it moved at all, their tests showed it only seemed to move as I moved. My movement forcing a sort of pumping action. Otherwise, the stuff that used to be human blood just sat immobile. Dr. Odensea speculated that the change of the fluid protected the inside of my body somehow, but he had not told me whether he had determined that to be true or not.

I sat on the metal table.

The techs, two new guys clearly nervous to be around me, grew even more nervous as they tried to stick needles in me.

I stayed still, only turning my head so I could see them better at their work.

One tech missed the vein several times. Finally, his hand shaking, he stepped back, eyes wide with fear.

"It is okay," I said. "I don't feel pain. You can keep trying until you hit the vein and get the fluid you need."

That did it. The man's eyes popped open even wider. All the blood drained from his face, and he fell to the floor.

The other tech stood staring at me with his mouth hanging open. He turned his head to look at his companion but made no move to check on the man. It was as though he was frozen in place.

I said, "I guess Dr. Odensea didn't tell you I learned how to talk."

The man looked back at me and shook his head, a weird sort of sound escaping his throat.

"Please, don't scream," I said, "He just fainted. He is fine. I can hear his heartbeat and breathing."

I reached out and took another syringe from the tray he held in trembling hands. I stuck it into the same place I'd been stuck with hundreds of other needles. Holding the needle steady, I inserted one vial until its rubber popped on the internal needle. I watched until the vial filled up with the green-black stuff that once was blood. With great care, I took the vial off the needle and laid it on the tray.

"Were you supposed to fill all of those?" I asked as I pointed to the five other vials on the tray.

The man took a deep breath and nodded. Then, as though coming to himself, he shook his head and set the tray down on another table. He approached me with a vial in one hand.

"I, er, no… We were not told you can talk," he said as he took over filling the vials. He kept his head turned away from me, focused only on the vial.

"I make you uncomfortable?"

The man lifted his shoulders in a shrug. "Yes… No. I knew we were going to be working with a docile zombie. That in itself is incredible. When we came in and saw you sitting here like any normal human, that was already shocking enough. I thought I had pissed someone off and I was being fed to you. I expected you to leap off the table and take a chunk out of me."

I looked away from the man.

"I haven't bitten a human in over a year," I said.

The man shifted beside me. The pop of another vial filled the silence.

A few moments later, the door opened and Dr. Odensea walked in. He glanced at the man still prone on the floor.

"Well, that didn't go so well. My apologies, Robert. I intended to tell you before you and Danny came in here but got caught up in some exciting results from another test."

The man he called Robert put the vial on the tray and looked at me, then at the doctor.

"Yeah, a heads up that this one is smart would have been great," he said, then he pointed at the tray. "Where do you want these, doctor?"

Dr. Odensea waved his hand dismissively. "Just take them to the lab. The gals in there will know what to do with them."

While Robert left the room, the doctor squatted next to the man on the floor. He patted the man on the cheek.

"Danny. Danny?"

The man moved his head from side to side. He blinked upward at the ceiling, then he seemed to recall where he was. He sat upright as though struck with electricity.

He pointed at me.

"That thing speaks!" he said, his voice shaking.

The doctor reached out and helped the man to his feet.

"Yes," he said, "This is Adam, the first of its kind that we know of. It is intelligent, speaks, learns, and is no threat to you."

Danny stared at me. Distrust flashed across his face. He looked at the doctor and shook his head.

"Nope. Not what I signed up for. I won't work with that thing. Absolutely not," he said. His face transformed. Instead of fear and shock, the light that filled his eyes was one of hate-fueled fire. The intensity in his stare made the doctor step between him and me.

"Okay, Danny. You go on back to the Colonel, then. You tell him exactly that. He'll reassign you somewhere else."

Danny shot the doctor a look. "You know he'll put me on the wall, or worse, on gathering patrol. That puts me outside the wall."

The doctor shrugged. His voice cold, he said, "You are more of a threat to Adam than Adam is to you. So, you cannot stay in my research facility. Now go. I'll call ahead so the Colonel will be expecting you."

Danny gave the doctor a look I was not familiar with before he turned and rushed out of the room.

The doctor looked at me, then at a folder in his hands.

"I have news to share with you, but I have to take care of that first."

He set the folder down and, with a promise to return in a short while, he left the room.

Once again, I sat and waited.

The analogue clock ticked. Michael had taught me how to understand the clock as a depiction of the passing of time. Time was a matter that was vaguely familiar. A barely-there memory, but I didn't understand why it mattered to humans. Still, I watched the minutes tick by, then the hour ticked past. Finally, almost two hours later, the doctor returned.

"Sorry about that, Adam," he said as he entered the room.

He approached me and made a face, seeing me sitting on the metal table.

Motioning to my room, he walked toward it. I stood and followed him. In my room, he clicked on his little remote, and the one wall I left bare changed from a view of somewhere overlooking a wide valley to a series of charts and medical images.

I glanced over them but had no way of understanding what I was seeing.

"Please, have a seat, Adam. This might take a while for me to explain. But I want to show you something."

I sat down on the bed while the doctor, folder in one hand and his remote in the other, manipulated one image to take the center of the wall.

"This is an image of human DNA," he said.

I looked at the way it spiraled on itself.

He clicked another image so that it sat side by side with the first.

"This is an image of your DNA," he said.

I stared at the two images. The human DNA was a perfect spiral. My DNA was similar, but it had gaps in some spots, and in two spots I saw a strange sort of branching off, like a thorn on a rose. I looked at the doctor, waiting for him to continue.

"As you can see, your DNA is basically human, but also, now, quite different. The missing part of your DNA is being sequenced. As are those strange extensions, that are unlike anything I have ever seen on a DNA sequence." He paused, and the images disappeared. He now pulled up an image of a fuzzy-looking ball with sucker looking appendages on it.

He pointed at it and said, "We found this in your tests. We almost missed it because it was so tiny. This is a pathogen. It is unlike anything we have ever seen. Completely new. We don't have enough to run tests on it, because it is in your body, but it is not prevalent. The most concentrated we have found it was in the samples we took of your spinal fluid. We need to take more spinal fluid, and I'd like to open you up and see if we can take a tissue sample from your brain."

I stared at him. So far, all the testing that had been done on me had been through fluid draws and tissue scrapings—skin samples, nails, hair, swabs of the inside of my mouth and nose. The doctor had not cut into me. He'd told me previously that it wasn't necessary because my organs had become necrotic and would not tell him anything anyway.

"You want to cut into my brain," I said. In a strange way, I felt hesitation. A new sensation. Earlier tests drew a kind of curiosity from me, but not fear, and not this feeling of reluctance. It was a strange feeling.

Dr. Odensea nodded. He turned to stare at the image of the pathogen. Then, he turned back to me and took a seat at the table.

"I do. I suspect the pathogen is the key to why you are different, and why you appear to still be changing. This is a thing called DNA methylation."

He paused and leaned toward me. "You realize you are still changing, don't you?"

"I am?" I asked. "No. I had not noticed."

He turned toward the wall and changed the glass to be reflective rather than a screen. Behind the doctor, I saw my reflection. I had not seen it since those first weeks in the facility. I stared at it before rising and approaching my reflection.

I had changed a lot.

Beyond the scrubs I wore, my skin had fully grown back. My cheeks were no longer sunken, gaunt, and so thin they were almost see-through. Now, they were thick and plump. My lips too. I opened my mouth. I no longer had many teeth, but the ones that remained sat in thick gums. The sores that had once filled my mouth and covered my ragged tongue were all gone. How strange that I could not feel these changes. That lack of feeling was going to be a danger to me. I looked at my nose. When I had come to the humans, my nose was rotten off. It had been gone, leaving an exposed look into the sinus cavity. Now, it was fully grown back. I turned my head from side to side, looking at it. Had it been like this when I was human?

I stepped even closer and looked into my eyes. Before, there had been no lashes, no eyebrows. The lids had been high and thin, because I did not need to blink to keep my eyes moist. While I still did not need to blink, I now had thick but short black lashes that curled upward away from my eyes. My brows were also thick and dark. The lids were no longer paper thin, but still stuck high from being dry.

And my eyes. They had been bloodshot and red, and the iris and pupil had been milky and foggy. My vision had not changed at all, but my eyes certainly had. Now, the whites were a soft lavender. Shockingly, even to me, my irises were purple with only the slightest specks of grey in them. The pupil was milky white, as though I was blind.

As I stood there, staring at my face, I reached up and ran a hand over my bald head. No hair had grown back.

I looked at the bare skin of my arms. There was no hair on my skin either. How strange. Shifting focus, I held out my hands. I had spent no time looking at my hands, so I had not noticed. Or if I had noticed I had thought nothing of it, but now, looking at my skin closely, I realized it too had changed, or was changing. It, too, had been paper-thin. Every black vein and artery had been clearly visible. The skin itself had been crinkled and dry. And so pale it appeared gray.

Now it was thick. The veins and arteries, still full of the thick sludge that had once been blood, were only visible in the crook of my elbow and along the top of my hands. The skin was no longer thin and dry. It was no longer pale gray, but blue-tinged. I looked upward at the light.

Dr. Odensea also looked upward and smiled. "No, it's not the lighting. That is your skin. And from our daily images taken of you, it is continuing to turn bluer."

I turned away from my reflection.

"I don't understand," I said.

The doctor nodded. "Neither do we, Adam. I suspect the pathogen is behind it, but I don't know for sure. I want to run more tests. But I need your permission to cut into your brain. You have never needed to be given anesthesia, pain blockers, but we have not broken your bones or cut into actual tissue. We will head into unknown territory, so we will need your complete approval, before, and if you agree to do it, then during the procedures as well."

I turned away from the doctor to take in the thing I was becoming.

"What am I?" I asked.

The doctor rose and moved to stand beside me. He was shorter than me. Had he always been shorter than me?

He made eye contact with my reflection and said, "I don't know. Can we find out together?"

CHAPTER EIGHT

THE FOLLOWING DAY, Dr. Odensea walked into my room with some of his staff behind him.

"Okay, Adam, let's get you prepped," he said without preamble.

I glanced about me, suddenly unsure.

"I'll watch the whole thing, Adam," Michael's disembodied voice echoed through the chamber.

Dr. Odensea nodded. "Michael will watch from my office. He thought it might remove any fears you might have."

I stood up and said, "I am not afraid. I don't feel fear."

The doctor stared at me a moment before he replied, "I know you think that to be true, but some of your hesitations and actions would state otherwise. At any rate, as I discussed with you yesterday, I'll also watch you closely to make sure I am not causing you pain. If you feel anything unpleasant, I will need you to tell me at once. Do you understand?"

"Yes," I said simply.

Dr. Odensea pointed to his staff and said, "Now, they will help you get prepped. We need to work in an entirely sterile manner to make sure the sample I take is not compromised. So, they will help you shower and clean and will get you on the surgical table. We'll strap you down again, entirely as a precaution."

He turned away from me and motioned to the others who came in to escort me to a room they called a bathroom, and into a plastic stall with running water they called a shower. After they scrubbed every inch of my body, they put a strange piece of fabric on me and loosely tied it at the back. They guided me to a padded table where they had me lie prone with my face in a strangely cushioned hole. I could see the floor, and the feet of the staff as they moved about the table. I tried to look up to observe the flurry of activity around me but couldn't move my head.

One of the female staff said, "We have your head tied down, so you won't move during the procedure."

"The rest of me?" I asked.

She replied, "A strap across your back and your knees, and then we have your wrists bound. If you get uncomfortable, please let me know. I will adjust them at once."

"I am fine," I said and continued to listen to the activity around me.

After a while, someone rolled a metal stool near my head. Feet appeared, and the person attached sat on the stool.

"Adam, one of the nurses is going to wash and prepare the area of your head that I'm going to cut into. Once that is done, I will begin the procedure. If you like, I can tell you what I am doing as we go," Dr. Odensea said.

"Yes," I said.

"Very well," he replied, and then he told someone to begin.

While the nurse began her work, Dr. Odensea vocalized the procedure.

"This is called a stereotactic brain biopsy, Adam. I am going to remove a small piece of tissue from your brain, but I'm also going to take a sample of your cranial blood vessels, and a sample of the dura matter, a membrane that encases your brain. We have already done all the three-dimensional mapping of your brain, so I know exactly where I want to insert the biopsy needle."

He paused, while the nurse stopped, stepped away, and returned with something that sloshed around in a container.

"Now, Adam, my nurse is making the site sterile with a special cleanser. You might smell the germicide."

I did. It was a harsh chemical smell that I also somehow seemed to taste. Bitter. Almost metallic.

Dr. Odensea spoke again. He said, "Now, ordinarily I'd give a patient medication to make them completely at ease. They have to be awake, you see. But that medication also blocks all the pain receptors. Curiously, while your nervous system seems to work, you do not feel pain, nor do you sleep, so I cannot use these medications without potentially harming you. I am using a marker to mark where I am going to cut your skull and insert the biopsy needle. I'm cutting into the skin with a scalpel and pushing the skin to the side so I can see the skull more clearly. You are going to hear the drill in just a moment. Are you ready?"

"Yes," I said.

Below me, I saw his feet shift as he moved his stool around to one side of my head. Just before the whirring of a drill came close to my ear, I heard a soft clink as something fell into a metal. When the drill bit into the bone of my skull, I felt some pressure on my head, but nothing alarming. There was a quick pop, and the drill stopped. The doctor's feet shifted him around farther, almost out of my line of sight.

"Interesting," he said in a faint voice.

"Doctor?" I asked.

"Just a moment, Adam, please," the doctor replied. To someone nearby, he said, "Make sure you zoom in on this. Move around from every angle. I want to review this later."

Other feet moved into view around my head, from one side all the way around to the other, causing the doctor to shuffle backward, away from me. After a moment, he shuffled back in and said, "Adam, your brain is unlike anything I have ever seen. On all the scans, it appears just as a human brain, but seeing it open with my own eyes... It's something quite extraordinary. Alarming, even."

Not knowing how to respond, I said nothing.

He continued, "We are filming this entire procedure. If you want to see it later, you can. But now, Adam, I am going to get a sample of the dura matter. Please tell me what you feel, if anything."

I waited in silence, listening to him as he directed his staff on what he wanted. I heard a tiny wet slap of sound but felt nothing.

"Did you feel that, Adam? I sliced the dura matter and cut off a tiny sample."

"I felt nothing," I said.

"Okay. I am going to insert the biopsy needle. Now that I am in here, would you be opposed to me taking multiple samples from distinct parts of your brain?"

I said nothing.

He said, "Let me see how this first sample goes. I will ask again to make sure you still feel no pain. Now. I'm inserting the needle into an area of your brain that allows you to comprehend sounds and language. Can you feel this?"

"No," I said.

"Very good. Okay. Almost done."

After a moment, the doctor shifted on his stool. He pushed away from me a little, then I heard something tap against plastic.

"The nurse is putting the sample into a dish that we can store it in. Now," he said, "You did not seem to feel anything there. How do you feel about me taking another four or five samples from other areas of your brain?"

I said, "Okay, Doctor."

"Very good. Very good," he said to me. To his staff, he said, "Bring me the other biopsy needles, and set up the portable scan machines. I'll need to do these in real time, coordinating as I go. Quickly, people. The longer his brain is exposed, the more likely we set it up for compromise."

I heard people rushing about for a few moments, until the doctor said, "Okay, Adam. Four or five more times. Are you ready?"

I remained silent.

He shifted closer to me, and whispered, "Please tell me if I end up hurting you. I will stop immediately."

"I will," I answered, and contented myself waiting.

Later, sitting alone in my cell, I stared at my reflection. A white bandage, wrapped around most of my head, reminded me of a picture in one of the children's books that Michael had brought to me. It was what he called a spooky story for kids set around a holiday people no longer celebrated. Children and even adults would dress up in costumes and wander about acting like scary things in exchange for sweet things called candy. Staring at the strange apparition of myself, I looked like the creature he called a mummy. Another undead thing. I had to wonder, if I could live undead, could all those other creatures, which humans called monsters, exist undead as well?

I understood enough about their lore and myths to know one reason I scared them so much was because, despite our presence, zombies should not be possible. Whatever I was compounded that impossibility with all the changes I was going through. Furthermore, if zombies existed, as I existed, then could these other monsters exist? Their mummies. Their vampires. Their half-human half-animal creatures like werewolves or sasquatch or whatever else that were not supposed to be possible.

I reached up and felt at the bandage, wondering how long it would have to be on. I didn't like it wrapped around my head the way it was. Unlike all the other things that had bound me since being among the humans, none of them made me uncomfortable like the bandage.

I wondered if I should tell Dr. Odensea.

Thinking about it for a few minutes, I decided to keep my discomfort with the wrap to myself.

Still running my fingers over the bandage, I worked a loose end free. I unwound the bandage and dropped it on the floor. One quick glance showed me there was no staining on the bandage. Had I been a human, the bandage would have been saturated with the blood that would have oozed from the wounds the doctor had inflicted to get his tissue samples.

I moved closer to the reflective part of the wall and stared at the spots where the doctor had cut into my skin. I felt the sutured areas and the barely detectable open holes left in the skull. Doctor Odensea had cut three more holes to avoid excess damage to my brain getting all these biopsies, though he expressed he was uncertain whether my brain could be damaged at all.

Something about regeneration. I heard one of his nurses mutter the word, drawing the doctor's attention to something she was seeing. He too had expressed initial shock. Apparently, it was happening more as they proceeded, which shocked him and his staff into silence while they did the last extractions.

I had an idea of what regeneration meant but wasn't entirely sure.

The door opened and Michael stood waiting there, staring at me, a strange look on his face.

"Hello, Michael," I said and turned to face him fully.

He waved me toward him and said, "I have to get you out of here."

"I am leaving?" I asked him.

With a strained look on his face, he nodded. "The settlement is under attack. We must go. Now."

The urgency in his voice reflected in the way his gaze darted around my cell. His eyes were wide, his jaw clenched, and his hands were in fists at his side. He seemed genuinely on edge.

"Danger?" I asked.

He waved at me impatiently and said, "Adam, really. We have to go. Now!"

I moved toward him, then paused. Turning to a shelf, I looked over the books. I wasn't concerned about the ones I'd already read. I knew them. But there were a few I hadn't read yet. Glancing over them, I reached out and grabbed the one I just started reading with Dr. Odensea. I held it tight in my hand. *Watership Down*. I moved out of the room and into a hallway. Michael stepped around me and took the lead.

"This way," he said as he ran toward a door at the far end of the hall.

CHAPTER NINE

MICHAEL OPENED THE DOOR, and we stepped onto a metal landing open to the outside. Below us, the humans were running about, loading things into vehicles, or rushing to protect the walls. On the walls, several of the humans were shooting down at something I couldn't see.

But I didn't have to see what the humans were shooting at.

I could hear them. Smell them.

Zombies.

A lot of them.

A horde.

A fleeting thought passed through my mind. Was it the horde I had been with?

Had I somehow brought them here?

I dismissed the idea. Zombies didn't track. They roamed. Mindlessly.

Michael ran down a set of stairs. I followed him. We reached the bottom and entered the rush of chaotic determination to get away, to survive.

There, the doctor was directing some of his staff to put some equipment into a special vehicle. A red vehicle. An ambulance. Before their world fell, these vehicles had been used to help save human lives.

Dr. Odensea glanced at me.

"You should have left that bandage on, Adam," he said. A slight frown revealed his dissatisfaction with me, but it was quickly replaced by a look of concern as one of his techs carried a heavy-looking box from inside.

"Careful with that," he cried out as he rushed to help with its weight. As he helped the tech place the box into the back of the ambulance, he called out to me and Michael.

"I want you both in this truck, now! We are leaving as soon as it is loaded."

Michael shook his head, "No way, doc. I'm going with my family."

Michael looked at me and said, "Adam, do you want to come with me and my family, or would you rather ride with the doctor?"

I stood watching them silently.

Michael was my friend. I know that meant something significant to humans. It did to me in a way too, but the doctor was also a friend, in an unusual way. A friend, if one is defined by the ability to trust someone else. I trusted Michael for certain. And I was growing to trust the doctor nearly as much. My hesitation was not so much about the idea of friendship, but more about my growing curiosity about myself.

Michael wanted to help me. I knew that. He wanted to protect me. At every new change brought my way, I'd seen him trying to.

But the doctor was looking for answers. Answers I was curious to know as well. Michael could not help me get those answers.

The doctor interrupted my thoughts.

"Adam, you go on with Michael. He will be part of the forward group. You'll be safer with him and that group. I'll meet you all at the rendezvous," he said before turning back to direct machine and box placement in the back of the ambulance.

Michael didn't wait; he took off running from the building we had just been in.

As the sounds of fighting gained intensity, I ran after him.

Trucks were parked against a metal gate to keep it from being forced open by the horde pressing on it from the outside.

Rage.

Hunger.

Single-minded madness.

I had been one of those creatures.

I still was.

But also, I was not.

I stopped running and just stared.

The scent coming off the zombies at the gate was overwhelming. How had I ever tolerated that stench before? Death. Rot. Sickness. Disease. Bile. It was sour and acidic in my nose and on my tongue.

Michael stopped and walked to my side.

"Is something wrong?" he asked, also staring at the raging mob outside the gates.

"I was that. I am that," I said.

"Does that make you feel something?" he asked, his eyes on my face.

"I don't know. Yes. No. The stench. It makes me feel something I don't know how to explain."

Michael moved around in front of me, blocking my view of the horde.

"Adam, you are not one of them anymore. In part, maybe, but most of you is different. And if the doc is right, then you are something entirely different now. Come on. I need to get my family out of here so the others can start moving out too."

"Just you and your family," I asked.

Michael started jogging off and called over his shoulder, "No. I am leading away all the young and elderly. They are our priority. We move them out first, away from the fighting. Away from the horde."

I ran after him.

We slowed down at a caravan of vehicles parked by another gate, one of solid metal with concrete braces against it. On the wall, men were shooting at the horde with arrows and slingshots instead of guns.

For the quiet. Not to draw more of the horde to that gate. I turned and looked around the settlement. All the other walls were noisy with gunfire and blasts from the little bombs they called grenades. The humans were killing a lot of zombies. The stench of their destroyed bodies filled the air. But for all they were killing, I could hear the strain on the walls. The horde was pressing hard. Driven by that rage and hunger, they would destroy each other to press those walls down. This mass of undead could level just about anything, given enough time. And those walls were running out of time.

I turned back to Michael.

He was helping kids and elderly into vehicles. Some people cried out at the sight of me, but Michael was quick to hush them, explaining I was the one that was being talked about in the settlement. I was the one that was different.

He called me a miracle.

An old woman walked over to me.

I could smell her age. Her body was riddled with disease gained from a long life. She had white hair, pulled back away from her face. Her eyes, slightly milky with age, were still vibrant and full of knowledge. Her brain was as healthy as any of the young ones already piled into the vehicles. I could sense that.

"So, you are the one they think can save us all," she said, her eyes boring up into mine.

I said nothing.

"Well, you are definitely different," she said. She reached out and poked at me. When I didn't move, she took one of my hands in hers.

"Well, come on then, whatever you are, help me into the truck."

I glanced at Michael, who was trying to hide a smile. But I let the woman lead me to the truck. She stopped and lifted her arms up.

As it dawned on me what she intended for me to do, I reached out and gripped her under her arms.

"Not so hard, you brute. You'll break me." She winced, and I lessened my hold on her and tested lifting her into the air. She clasped my forearms with her hands and held on while I twisted to set her in the back of a box truck lined with seats.

"Hmph… not bad, whatever you are," she said. I let her go, but she leaned toward me and whispered in my ear, "I'm Sam, dear. You remember that. I don't care what anyone else says about you. I think Michael is right. You may be exactly what this world needs to heal."

Without another word, she turned away from me and sat down.

"Adam," I heard Michael call.

I moved around to where he was waiting beside the first truck.

"Can you please open that gate? Wait until we are all through, then close it behind us. The last truck, driven by my wife, will stop for you."

I said nothing but moved to do as Michael asked.

Pulling the solid metal gate back against the wall, I realized the humans on the wall had done their part. There were no zombies left here. I looked up at the wall to see many of them peering down, some with their weapons trained on me.

Michael drove through. Then the next vehicle. Then the next, and the next until all were through. I watched them all move on down the rough track except for a small truck that stopped.

A woman leaned out the window and called out in a low voice, "Hurry, Adam. Close the gate, and let's go!"

I pulled the gate to close it. As I did, a horrible screeching sounded from across the settlement. I stopped as a section of the wall, cobbled together from whatever scraps of metal and wood the settlement found at its creation, bent inward.

It would have held up fine against a few zombies here and there, or even a smaller horde, if it had been spread out. The wall was not strong enough for a horde this size, clustered as it was. The weight of the horde pushed it over and down.

As zombies pooled into the settlement, I shifted my focus to where the doctor and his staff were still working to load things from the concrete building.

I turned to the woman in the truck and waved her on.

"Go!" I said.

She stared at me for a moment, then looked at the reflection in the side mirror of the vehicle. I knew she saw what was making me stay. She looked back at me, her lips pressed together in a grim line.

"Help them," she said, "if you can."

She shifted her vehicle into gear and drove after the caravan. I watched as the distance grew, a strange knotting inside my stomach as they moved further away from the chaos that raged behind me. The cries of terror and pain snapped me back to the present, and I shut the gate quickly.

I ran toward the doctor to help.

Dr. Odensea was still madly directing people about as they tried to focus on moving out despite the increasing danger surging their way.

I reached him just as the people who had been trying to hold the wall did. Each of them, armed with guns, knives, axes, and whatever else they could use, fought like animals against the surging wave of raging zombies. I had to admire them. Men and women, young and old, they all fought bravely.

One woman saw the doctor and called out, "You have to get out of here. We can't leave until you and your staff do."

As she finished her command, a zombie grabbed at her. Its hands tried to grip her, its gaping mouth trying to get a bite, its head lowering closer and closer even as she struggled to get her blade arm free. Unable to lift her arm, she pushed against the monster, holding it as far from her as she could.

I knew it was a losing battle. Zombies were strong. Dead weight in every push. It was difficult to disentangle from their grip. I rushed around the doctor, grabbed the zombie by its shoulders, and yanked it off the woman. She staggered backwards, her eyes wide, instantly checking her shoulders and upper arms for bite marks.

Zombie still in my hands, its attention now on me, I watched its rage blossom even more as it tried to attack me. Without thinking, I let go with one hand. Punching straight out, my fist shattered what remained of its face. My fist crashed through rotten flesh and facial bone until it rested in soft brain matter. There, I grabbed a handful of that strangely half-dead, half-alive mass and yanked it out. The zombie fell limp at my feet.

I stared down at it as I shook the brain from my hand.

"My god," the woman said in a faint voice beside me.

I looked at her, then at the doctor.

"Must go," I said.

The doctor stared at me, a bemused and horrified expression on his face.

"Still a monster," I said to him, and he shook his head, though I could not fathom the meaning of the gesture.

He turned to continue directing people, ignoring my statement that we needed to leave.

The woman stepped around me, half her attention on the fighting that still raged around us. "Get the doc out of here, right now," she said to me. I can't afford to lose any more of these people."

I glanced at her before I let my gaze roam the entire settlement. The wall had been pressed inward in several more spots, and the remaining humans were backing toward a bank of vehicles near where I was with the doctor.

They'd be overwhelmed before long. As it was, they were losing more and more people, and from the smell of fresh blood, I knew they'd lose more to the change along the way.

I turned to the doctor. Grabbing him around the waist, remembering that I nearly injured the old woman with my strength, I lifted him from the ground and put him in the back of the ambulance. Grabbing the door, I climbed up beside him, one hand on his chest to keep him in place. I called to the front of the vehicle to the man in the driver's seat, "Go!"

The man ignored my command. Instead, he looked at the doctor. The doctor looked at me, at my hand on his chest. The hand with the brain remnants still on it.

He called out, "Get us out of here, James."

With a heavy sigh, he brushed my hand away. Working his way to the front of the ambulance, securing equipment as he went, he finally settled on the front of the gurney and stared out the front of the vehicle as the driver sped across the compound to another gate.

As we slammed through it, the gate splintered into pieces. While the doctor stared forward, I looked out the small back windows. Already, the woman was directing people to vehicles to make their own getaway. But one by one, more humans fell under the zombie rush.

Somehow, amazingly, the woman fought off several more before she grabbed onto the side of a large boxlike vehicle. Clinging to it, she smashed and slashed as the vehicle moved to follow the others out of the settlement.

Once I saw the vehicle free of the gate, I turned to face the front as well.

I did not know where we were going, but I knew my place among the humans had changed.

We traveled without stopping until the engine of one of the caravan vehicles could go no further. Most of the people that were with us used the time to get out and stretch. A lot grieved. Many expressed fears of finding a new place to settle.

Listening to their conversations as I sat on the edge of a flatbed truck, I learned that the settlement had stood fast from the beginning of the change. That was no small feat.

Questions rang out. Why was this horde different?

Some speculated it was as though the horde was driven.

I listened more closely to that conversation.

"I tell you, even at the beginning, the zombies never moved so fast, nor with that much aggression," one man said.

A woman replied, "They've always been aggressive. Mad."

The man argued, "No. I'm telling you; this attack was different. Didn't you notice how they pushed on?"

She said, "Yeah. So?"

The man sighed and said, "Think back to when we were in Albany. When the camp was attacked there. When a zombie fell one of us, it stopped. It didn't move on. It stayed with the human it was feeding on. That was predictable. Because they were so singularly driven to feed, we knew that for every one of us that fell, three or more of them would go into a feeding frenzy on the fallen and fewer were left to attack."

Shivering, the woman nodded. "Isn't that how the governor ended up saving his refugee camp? By having volunteers sacrifice themselves so the healthy, the young, could get away?"

The man said, "Yes. Because it was predictable behavior. This attack, this was not zombie behavior. They didn't stop and frenzy over the fallen."

I got off the back of the truck and approached the couple.

"Are you certain?" I asked.

The man and woman both paled as I approached.

"Stay away," said the man, pulling out his blade and holding it toward me.

The woman jumped to his side, her eyes wide, her blade also drawn. "You... You... You talk!" she said.

The man squinted at me and slightly lowered his blade. "They said you were something different. Look at you. Not like them anymore. Not like us either."

I ignored his observations.

"The zombies were not feeding?" I asked, staring at the man.

"No. They were not feeding," he said.

I turned away from him. Where was the doctor? I scanned the caravan of vehicles, until I discovered him far down toward the back, bent over someone lying on the ground.

I rushed toward him, and saw he was stitching up a wound on one of the human's arms. As I approached, he looked up at me.

"Ah, Adam," he said, no warmth in his greeting. He seemed upset that I forced him into the ambulance. He turned back to the person's arm and finished stitching the wound.

He stood up and faced me. "Something I can help you with?"

I said, "The horde. It didn't feed."

His eyes shot to my face. "They didn't feed. Of course they did. They always do."

"No. A man and a woman said they bit and moved on. Like they were herded. Not hungry," I said.

Dr. Odensea looked past me at people milling about. Stepping around me, he stopped one young man and asked, "When people fell, did the zombies feed?"

The young man nodded, but then he stopped. Cocking his head to the side, his gaze distant as he faced back the way we had come, he finally shook his head. "No. I don't think they did. I saw my friend fall. Two bit him, but when he fell, they moved on and tried to attack one of the other guys."

That fact didn't seem to bother the young man. Once he was finished speaking, he turned away from the doctor and continued with his task.

The doctor moved along the caravan, asking random people what they saw during the attack.

All the answers were the same. Disturbingly the same. The zombies did not feed.

When we were near the front of the line, the doctor turned and looked at me. "What does that mean, Adam?" he asked.

I stared at him.

After a moment, I said, "I don't know, but it is bad."

CHAPTER TEN

OUR SMALL CARAVAN moved on for several days. The day we were supposed to rendezvous with Michael and his group, we pulled into an enormous field. Most of it was concrete, with tufts of grass growing up in a myriad of cracks. At first, the group waited in the center of the concrete area, but as the day wore on, people got nervous.

James, the driver of the ambulance, was talking animatedly to the doctor while I sat on the ground waiting to be tasked with something to help the people. Voices raised, allowing me to hear them even from a distance.

"Absolutely not, James. It is entirely out of the question. We can't spare anyone else. You heard what our scouts said. Another horde is nearby. We may have to run again," the doctor said in a strained voice.

"I'm telling you; we need to stay here until Michael's group arrives. Why don't we ask Tamra?" James snapped back, the level of his voice matching the doctor's.

"Ask me what?" asked Tamra, the woman who'd been directing the humans in the settlement. I wondered about her. She differed from the men, yet she carried at least as much authority as any of the men I had met so far.

James turned to her. While he lowered his voice, a seemingly forced calm put an edge to it as he said, "I think we should move our group into the stadium. There are only two sets of gates to hold. We can bar up one, and be set to run out the other, if necessary, but I tell you nothing is getting in if we want to stay here a bit. We have a lot of wounded who need time to heal. Plus, it's safer in there while we wait for Michael."

Tamra looked at the doctor. "You think it's a bad idea?"

Dr. Odensea, his voice so low I could barely hear it, said, "We have not cleared the stadium. We can't afford to lose anyone right now trying to clear it. There is no telling what is inside those gates."

Tamra looked across the concrete field toward the tall gates that sealed the thing they called a stadium. I turned my attention to it as well.

It was impressive. It was large, tall, and round. Much taller than the buildings in the settlement. Some areas of it were taller still, with expansive windows reflecting the surrounding area. While I observed it, I waited for Tamra to respond.

After a moment, she did.

"I agree. We can't afford to send anyone in there. We are spread too thin as it is..."

James interrupted, "But we are sitting ducks out here!"

Tamra raised a hand and waited for James to calm back down. Then she said, "but I also agree that if we could clear the stadium, it would be safer for us to rest within those thick walls and heavy gates. At least until Michael catches up."

Dr. Odensea shrugged as he said, "So we are at an impasse."

Tamra shook her head.

"I don't think so," she said, and she glanced over her shoulder to look at me. "We can send him."

I got to my feet. While I walked toward them, the doctor leveled all kinds of arguments to keep me from going into the structure. He got more irate the closer I got. Finally, I stood with the three, and the doctor fell silent.

"Adam, we could use your help..." started Tamra.

"I know," I said, "I heard."

Her eyes widened, but she nodded and continued, "Would you be willing to go in there and see if it is safe for us to move in until Michael comes?"

Dr. Odensea stepped toward me and said, "You don't have to do this, Adam. You are one of a kind. If anything happened to you..."

James rolled his eyes to the side. "For god's sake, doc, the thing ain't even human!"

The doctor turned to him angrily, "No! He's not human. He is different. And you want to put this incredible creature in danger for no good reason?"

James threw up his hands and stormed away, practically yelling backward, "Once again, doc, your science is more important than the people you claim you want to save."

I watched the younger man storm off, then I turned to Tamra. "What do I have to do?"

Tamra smiled slightly.

"Are you brave or stupid?" she asked, but then she shook her head. "Never mind, I don't mean that. Come on. I will show you where to go in. As we walk, I'll tell you what to do."

She started away, but the doctor stepped in front of me, genuine concern in his scrutiny.

He said, "I know you feel no pain, and I know human concepts of some things are still strange to you, but don't put yourself at risk. If it is too much, get out. Save yourself. Do you understand?"

I looked into his eyes and nodded. "I think so. Save myself, like I saved you."

A peculiar look flashed across his face, but it passed. He took a deep breath before hitting me on the arm with a smile.

"That you did, Adam," he said, "and I have been ungrateful. Please. Be careful in there."

I said nothing more as I stepped around him to follow Tamra.

Along the way, she told me what to look for. As we reached a door to one side of the gate, she stopped and looked up at me. "The main thing is, we can't be in there if zombies are.

Go in. See how many there are. If there are not a lot, kill them. If there are too many, come back out. We will stay out here."

I said nothing. When she stepped back from the door, a hand on the blade tucked in her belt, I knew it was time for me to go in.

I yanked the door open. Staring into the gloom beyond, I stepped inside.

Tamra shut the door behind me, cutting off all the natural light. Regardless, I could see everything in the immediate area with no problem.

The room was devoid of both human and zombie. I moved across the small space to another door, this one solid metal. I opened it.

Screeching hinges shattered the silence, and I stopped to listen. If any zombies were near enough to hear the high-pitched sound, they'd make noise as well.

Silence.

I stepped through the door, shutting it behind me, though I was not sure why. Looking around, I realized I was in a long, concrete hall that gently sloped upward. Cocking my head to the side, I listened.

Scuffling of small creatures. Mice or rats, like the ones the doctor had in his lab. Maybe birds nesting somewhere nearby. Papers rustling in a draft that wafted over me from somewhere along the hall. But no other sounds.

Looking up the hall, I could see spots of light filtering in at various places.

Looking the other direction, I saw only darkness.

I turned toward the dark.

Not far along that route, the floor leveled out. To one side was the gate that led to the concrete field where the people were. On the other side, another gate of metal rods that were as thick as the smallest part of my arm, blocked the way. Beyond that, I could smell dirt, plastic, and paint. I walked to the metal bars and pressed on them, but I could not get them to move. When I looked down, I noticed the bars extended into the ground. I turned around and went back to the hall. It continued past both gates. I stared into the darkness of the empty hall. Everything remained silent.

As I wandered along the hall, I found many remnants of humanity. Papers. Toys. Trash. Decaying remnants of a time long gone.

Doors were scattered here and there.

I opened each one and looked inside. Listening. Smelling.

Each room sat empty and silent.

Finally, I reached the end of the hall, and the second gate James had mentioned. It was exactly like the first one, with gate leading to the outside world, and a set of metal bars leading to the smell of soil.

Ahead of me, the hall sloped upward.

That was when I heard it.

Muffled shuffling or shifting of something somewhere ahead.

Then came the smell. That rancid, sickly sweet stench of rot.

The hall sloped ever upward, leveling out in various spots to short halls leading further into the structure. I passed most of them, intent on finding the source of the sounds and smell.

At the third one, I stopped. The stench was overpowering. I turned down the short hall and realized it opened to the interior of the structure. Below, a large circle of soil was spread out. Faded paint on the dirt showed lines that led from one little cream-colored plate to another. Four of them in all, making a sort of square shape. I stared out over the open space.

Shuffling sounded to the side.

I turned my head and saw it.

The creature sat in the middle of a long row of chairs. One of dozens running up the inside of the structure—a strange, tiered view almost dizzying to behold.

Its attention fixed on me; the zombie reached out toward me but stopped. I didn't smell like food. After all, I was undead as well.

I walked closer to it.

Long, light hair clung to the creature's head. Limp and dirty, but still there. The creature itself was tied to the chair.

A wide piece of fabric wrapped several times around it, tied in the front in a sturdy knot.

This once-human had come in here and tied itself to the chair.

I stared at the creature. It stared back at me.

The realization of just how much I had changed over the past few months hit me. Not that long ago, I was that creature. Unable to process anything but the smell and taste of flesh to abate the internal roaring rage. As it jerked unwillingly against the knotted fabric, its head and hands shaking uncontrollably, I realized it was starving. Not that it would die, but a starving zombie reacts differently to things than sated ones do.

A tight feeling crept up on me.

Turning my attention to the wide-open space in front of the zombie, I searched for others. I heard none. Smelled none. Just this one. The tightness intensified.

I turned back to the creature and undid the knot that held it in the chair. It lunged upward, too weak to move me, but still crashing into me to find relief for its hunger.

Instinctively, I thrust my arm out, right into the creature's mouth.

It bit down. Then it flung itself away from me, back into the chair. A new wildness about it. Its deep red eyes bored into mine, almost an expression.

Then I understood. The creature was afraid. Of me.

I stepped toward it. I wanted to lead it out; allow it to escape.

Pity. That was what I was feeling. Michael had described it to me. I pitied the starving creature in front of me. I had no fear of it. I'd hoped if it fed off me, it would sate its rage, and I could lead it out of the structure away from the humans who would surely kill it without another thought.

But as the zombie stood before me, trembling with rage and fear, I realized it would not feed off me, which meant I would not be able to lead it out.

I had no choice.

Snapping my arm out, as I had with the zombie that had attacked Tamra, I smashed my fist into the creature's face and damaged the brain. The creature went limp. I pulled my hand out and shook off the gore.

The feeling of pity was replaced by another sensation deep inside. This one hurt. It made me want to run away from the creature in the chair, and from the humans who had expected me to kill it.

The silence of the large space wrapped around me as I stood there trying to understand the battling emotions within me.

High above me, I noticed the tiniest pricks of holes in the ragged canopy that covered the open space. Though the holes, I could make out just the faintest remnants of light.

It was night. I'd been in the structure for too long.

Ignoring the unanswered questions bubbling in my mind, I rushed down to the gate where I knew Tamra was still waiting.

The blackness of the halls swallowed me, making me pause. I had no fear of the dark. Not with my eyes, ears, and nose as powerful as they were. To fear the dark was not sensible. To fear anything was insensible. Still, the blackness was increasingly hard for me to navigate despite my senses.

Finally, I reached the lower level and rushed across the hall to the gate.

I pounded five times and waited.

Nothing.

Tamra had told me to pound five times. She would hear it, and pound back three. Then and only then, I was to open the gate to let the group in.

But no one pounded back.

I pounded harder, five times. Then I pressed my ear to the gate.

There was movement beyond the gate. Voices calling. No. Screaming.

I pounded again, even harder.

As I pounded the gate, a metal bar shook in its holdings. Seeing it, I realized it was holding the gate shut. Dismissing my directions, I removed the bar and tossed it to the side. I pulled back on one of the big metal doors.

Screaming filled my ears. Smoke filled my nose. And the scent of copper. The scent of death.

Standing at the gate, I stared out at the concrete field. The humans were in a circle, trying to fight back against a rush of zombies. In the middle of the circle was the ambulance and the tent where the wounded were being cared for.

From where I stood, I could see the zombies were still coming from beyond the concrete.

Without waiting, I rushed to the humans, knocking several zombies to the ground as I went.

"Get inside," I said to Tamra as I stepped up to the humans, crushing a creature as I spoke.

She glanced at me for a split second, then beyond me to the gaping gate.

"Hurry. Everyone. Help a wounded. Get in that gate. Now! Go!" she screamed as she stepped forward to make a clearing for the others.

I stood beside her and fell another creature. Then another. A fist into the face. A fist downward onto the skull. Behind me, the noises of concerted efforts to move people drove the zombies in front of me into an even worse frenzy. One got past me and advanced on one of the younger women. Without thinking, I reached toward it and grabbed it by its arm. While the limb came off with the tiniest yank, the creature still moved toward the woman.

The woman turned toward the creature, unflinching. In slow motion, she lifted her arm high and brought it down fast, slamming a blade into the top of the creature's head.

She glanced up at me and shrugged before she turned back to help one of the walking wounded.

I went back to help Tamra, who was struggling to keep several creatures from breaking through to the people behind us. Noting that the others were already well on their way to the gate, I said to her, "You should get in the ambulance and drive it inside. There is a lot that the people can use. I'll cover you as you go."

She looked at me, stabbed a zombie in the eye, and turned to the open front door of the ambulance. As soon as the door was closed, the zombies shifted their attention to the people moving into the structure. As one, they moved toward the gate, completely ignoring me. I walked among them, moving to their front lines, taking out one after another.

Tamra zoomed past me and into the stadium.

The metal hinges screeched as people drew the gate inward.

Someone called out to me, "Adam! Come on!"

I walked faster, leaving the shuffling creatures behind me, slipping through the gate just as it was about to close all the way.

Inside, several people struggled to pick up the heavy metal beam.

I approached and lifted it easily. After dropping it into the brackets that originally held it, I pressed against the heavy metal door.

The zombies pressed up against it already. I could sense them. But the door didn't budge. It didn't even creak.

The people were safe. For now.

CHAPTER ELEVEN

THAT FIRST NIGHT, the humans camped right there behind the gate. They were all used to the sounds of the zombies outside, and it was easier to set up immediate camp there rather than explore the structure for themselves in the dark.

"What is this place?" I asked the doctor. The broken images of those distant memories plagued me.

"It was a stadium. Here, groups of people formed teams and played a game we called baseball. It was a popular game." He paused for a moment, before he said, "I'm surprised this one appears in such good shape. After the change, most of the big arenas and stadiums were used to quarantine or trap the zombies. They were burned or bombed to kill everything inside. You said you only found one?"

"Yes. It tied itself to a chair up there," I said and pointed upward.

"Interesting," said the doctor. "When it was human, it must have gotten bit. Few knew at first that there was no cure and no coming back from it. When people realized what was really happening, they often killed themselves, to either not get bit, or to not change after getting bit. I suppose this person was too afraid to kill themself."

Not knowing what to say, I sat in silence. I didn't think the doctor would react well if I told him I was hoping to let the creature go. But then he reached out and grabbed my arm.

"What happened here?" he asked as he pointed to bite marks from the creature.

"It bit me," I said.

"It bit you?" he asked. Immediately, he was on his feet.

"Come with me, right now," he said.

With a flashlight guiding him, he led the way to the ambulance, which he had converted into a moving laboratory. He stepped inside and motioned for me to follow. He pointed for me to sit on one end of the gurney while he got swabs and syringes to take tests.

I sat still while he took his samples. Swabs from the bite. He said he wanted a sample of its saliva. He took that sample plus more of my skin around the bite, from the wound itself, and from other areas of my body.

He seemed really concerned.

"Doctor?" I asked.

He paused as he was moving samples to slides for viewing under his machine he called a microscope.

"Adam, you are a new thing. What if a zombie bite can turn you back? What if you are infected now? With your new strength and healing abilities, what will that look like? You are still undead. For now, I need you to promise me you'll stay in this vehicle. No matter what. Until the virus in that creature's saliva has turned you or dies. Do you understand?"

"Yes," I said. "I don't want to put you at risk. Or anyone here. Maybe I should wait outside the gates?"

He shook his head. "No. I will watch you closely. If I see you change, then we will discuss that again."

Without another word, he left the ambulance and shut it up tight. I heard him tell James and Tamra just at the back of the vehicle, and they agreed that keeping me locked up was for the best.

The doctor left me alone for a long time. Waiting in solitude, I listened to the activity of the humans outside the ambulance. They settled in for the night, with only a few on watch. At various points, the shuffle of feet across concrete alerted me to a change in watch as the hours passed. Then the sounds of people waking, eating, talking, and moving about filled the silence. I couldn't make out what anyone was saying, but they sounded calm. Relaxed.

Finally, the doctor came into the ambulance. He turned on bright lights, ignoring me in his single-minded focus on something he was researching. I said nothing. I simply watched.

His head bent over his microscope and placed a little glass slide onto the device. He peered through the tube at one slide after another, taking notes as he went.

A harsh pounding on the back door of the vehicle made him jump, and he nearly hit his head on the equipment he had stashed overhead.

"What?" he yelled toward the door.

The door opened and Tamra peered in. She nodded curtly to me, then focused on the doctor.

"Doc, there is something I think you need to see," she said.

He frowned at her and said, "I'm busy, Tam. Can it wait?"

Tamra looked at me, then back at him. Her voice was flat as she said, "No. It can't. We found the zombie Adam said he killed. There is something odd about it."

Dr. Odensea got up and stared at me, then at Tamra.

"Should Adam come?" he asked her.

"Might not be a bad idea. Maybe he knows something about it."

The doctor turned to me. I could see he was hesitant to let me leave the ambulance. He reached out and looked at my arm. It was completely healed. He looked at me, leaning so close I could still smell the food he ate for breakfast.

"Come on, Adam. You are okay. Let's see this creature you killed."

He hopped down from the ambulance and hurried after Tamra. I moved to follow them. Not long after, we were standing over the zombie's slumped body. The change in the area since the humans moved in was remarkable. Daylight streamed into the space that had previously been pitch black, with only patches of light shining through. I glanced upward.

The humans had already climbed up. Vast sheets of metal had been slid back to the sides of the structure. Now it was open to the sky, where the night before only the tiniest bits of sky could be seen.

Rich black soil sat among the lines of paint and the flat disks I had seen. As the sun shone down, I realized this was a place the humans might decide to stay. They relied on growing food. The soil here was rich with nutrients; the smell coming from it earthy and damp.

Murmurs from Tamra and Dr. Odensea drew my attention back to them. They stood bent over the zombie, looking at something I couldn't see. From where I stood, I noticed nothing unusual, although something smelled different. I looked around, trying to place the source of the scent. It came from the body.

I leaned closer and smelled more deeply. It was like the soil out in the open area.

Tamra lifted her head and looked at me.

"Adam, have you seen anything like this before?" she asked.

"Like what?" I asked.

She waved me closer to where she was and pointed to a cavity in the creature's body. I hadn't seen it when I freed the creature from its self-imposed bonds, but there it was, a gaping hole in her abdomen. The ragged shirt must have covered it before.

I peered down into the hole. And stared some more.

Far back, near the creature's spine, was something. Something pale, almost blue in color.

The doctor pulled out a flashlight and shined it on the pale object.

"My god," he said, his voice shaking. "The creature was pregnant as a human. How awful. That must be the unborn child."

He reached in to grab at the thing, but I stopped him with a quick snap of my arm, grabbing his wrist just shy of the hole.

"No. Not dead," I said simply, watching the tiny thing.

Tamra stood upright.

She said, "What? What do you mean it's not dead? Adam, you pulled its damn brain right out of its head! No zombie can survive that."

The doctor, his wrist still in my hand, was staring at the object too.

In awe, he said, "Tamra, he doesn't mean the zombie. He means the baby."

Tamra gasped, and in my peripheral vision, I saw her head snap toward the unborn child.

"Like hell..." she muttered.

She pulled a small blade from her belt and held it out.

"We best destroy it. And don't tell any of the others. I don't think any of them have ever seen a zombie baby. It would shatter some of the women, I think," she said.

"No," I said. "Not zombie."

I pointed at the little creature, and then at my skin. The hue was the same.

Tamra stood back upright, as did the doctor. They stared at me with expressions I could not interpret.

I looked back at the small thing. It had not moved. It made no sound. Yet, somehow, I knew it was like me: it was dead, but aware.

Without waiting for the doctor or Tamra to decide, I reached into the dead zombie's stomach and picked up the tiny creature. I held it in my hands and pulled it toward me, looking at it from one side, then another. Finally, I slipped a finger under its tucked chin and lifted gently.

A short squeak sounded, making Tamra and the doctor shudder beside me.

But I was staring into lavender eyes with purple irises and white pupils just like mine.

―

Back in the ambulance, I held the tiny thing in my hands. Sensations filled me that I was completely unprepared for. Sensations that were almost like memories yet also new and strange.

The little thing did not move. Like me, it was still. But its eyes bored into mine. It was unsettling in many ways, yet also thrilling.

Dr. Odensea sat beside me, staring at it in silence.

Tamra had still wanted to kill it. I knew the doctor initially felt the same way, but I refused to give it to either of them. As Tamra got more determined to destroy the little one, I decided and voiced it. I told her she'd have to kill me to kill it.

I had not expected her reaction. She had instantly deflated despite a threatening flash in her eyes. Instinctively, I clutched the tiny thing higher on my chest. Tamra breathed in deeply and shook her head. She pointed at the creature and told me it was my responsibility. But she told me I had to keep it hidden until I was back in the ambulance. She was determined no one else should know of its existence. The doctor had agreed.

The doctor brought me back to the present when he reached out and touched the creature gently.

"I would like to test its tissues, Adam," he said simply.

I looked at the man but said nothing.

He continued, "I want to see if it is like you. And I want to figure out if I can tell why it is like you, as I suspect from its coloring and stillness it is. Does it not feel pain?"

I gently squeezed the creature's toes. It showed no reaction.

"No pain," I said.

"Are you certain?" Dr. Odensea asked.

I looked at him. He was staring at the creature, a look of fear and wonder on his face. I felt a sudden understanding of what he seemed to be feeling. Shifting my attention back to the little bluish thing in my own blue-tinged hands, I too, wondered.

"Where do you want me to place it so you can take a sample?" I asked. A sudden eagerness to learn about this creature created a bubbly feeling inside me.

The doctor got up and laid out a white sheet on a clear part of the table where he'd been looking at slides. He waved me toward it.

I placed the thing in the center of the small space, and leaned on the table, noting how the thing was just a little wider than my hand, almost double my hand's length, and almost fat looking.

The doctor murmured as he jotted down notes on a notepad.

"Was this creature a zombie in its mother's womb? Did it draw nourishment from its mother even after she changed? Did this change begin naturally, or was it triggered? What was the trigger? Will this creature show the same characteristics as Adam? Will this creature grow? Is it, like Adam, intelligent?"

After he was done writing his notes, he pulled out a long strip with numbers on it. He placed one end at the head of the creature and stretched it to the creature's toes. He wrote something on the notepad.

"Will it bite me if I touch around its face?" he asked me.

"I don't know," I said.

I put my finger by its mouth. Its eyes just continued to stare into mine, but it did not react in any other way.

"Do you want me to do something?" I asked Dr. Odensea. "It does not want to bite me."

The doctor nodded and handed me the strip.

"You saw how I held the tape by the head and stretched it to the toes? I need you to hold the end there on one shoulder... Yes. Just like that. Now stretch it tight to the other shoulder. Hold it. Okay. Thank you."

He wrote something else on his notepad, before directing me to wrap the strip around the creature's head and hold it until he got what he called a cranial measurement and wrote it down.

"Why the measurements?" I asked him as he put the strip he called a measuring tape away.

"You and I will do these every day. These will help us determine if the creature is growing," he said. He reached overhead and pulled out a flat white device. Setting it next to the creature, he asked me to place the creature on it. When I did, a small screen was activated with a bunch of numbers.

"What are those?" I asked.

"That is the creature's weight. Also, to help us see whether it is growing or not."

"What does it mean if it grows?" I asked, staring down at it.

Dr. Odensea cleaned the device and put it back in the overhead cabinet before he replied. He leaned against the table, staring off into the distance as he was thinking.

Finally, I picked up the creature and moved back to the bench, where I sat with it in my arms. The movement caught the doctor's attention.

He turned to the table and, after collecting the small items, he sat beside me.

"I don't know, Adam. To be honest, I'm baffled by its existence. As you baffle me. And by zombies. None of this makes any sense, yet here we are. I have an idea, though. Taking some samples from the creature might help me find some answers."

Carefully, he reached out and took the thing's little foot.

He glanced up at me as he held a scalpel near the foot. "Adam, I promise, if this seems to cause the thing pain, I won't take any more. Okay?"

I looked at the man. "Okay," I said back, and stared in fascination, and maybe a touch of fear, as the doctor scraped a small layer of skin off the thing's foot. He placed the sample in a small dish and turned to stare as the tiny wound was already closed and new skin appeared. The doctor sat back; his eyes wide in apparent surprise.

"That is healing faster than any of your wounds did."

He rushed to his microscope and cut an even smaller sample to place on a slide. I watched him bend over the machine and stare into the tubes.

"Adam, I think you made this thing," he said, his voice barely louder than a whisper. He sat back and swiveled on the stool to look at me. "The creature's tissue is a part of its own, and it looks like some of yours."

He reached out and grabbed my arm where the zombie had bitten me. The bite mark was nearly gone. Only a thin white line showed where it had been.

"I have an idea," he said as he let my arm drop.

He was out of the ambulance in a flash, shutting the door in a hurry, and disappearing from view.

I stared after him for a bit until the tiny thing in my hands gave the tiniest squeak. I looked down at it, to find it still staring at me.

"I'm Adam," I said.

After that, we just sat in silence, staring.

CHAPTER TWELVE

THE CAMP WAS QUIET. From the lack of light in the front of the ambulance, I could tell it was night. Dr. Odensea had not returned since his hasty departure. I wondered if I should go look for him. Just as I was about to place the creature in a small tray that I found under the bench, the back door opened and the doctor, James, and Tamra stared in at me. A few fires were burning in metal buckets and metal trash cans, but everyone was asleep except the three staring up at me.

"Adam, would you come with us?" Tamra asked.

I didn't hesitate. I could tell from their smells; they were anxious about something. Was it another zombie? Did I miss one?

I set the creature down on the tray and set it where I had been sitting.

"Is that thing okay to be left alone?" Tamra asked.

"What is it?" asked James.

"Never mind," said the doctor as I hopped down. He shut the door firmly behind me and locked it with a key.

James threw the doctor a severe look, but then looked at me as he said, "This is crazy. I can't believe you want to try this."

Tamra moved away from us, into the room that led to the door by which I had originally entered the stadium. Once we were in the room, each of them lit flashlights. Tamra shut the door behind her and led the way to the next room, and to the door leading outside.

"Adam, we want to let just one zombie in here. We need you to help us capture it," Dr. Odensea said.

"Capture a zombie," I said.

"Crazy," said James, as he stood behind the door, ready to brace it against a rush.

"Can you hear them out there?" Tamra asked.

I listened.

"Yes. But they seem to have moved away," I said.

"Okay. Then we will have to draw one's attention," she said. "I'll go out and see what's what."

"No," I said.

The three looked at me.

"I can see in the dark. Your flashlight will draw too many. That door won't hold like the big metal ones. I will go find one. I will bring it back."

Tamra looked at James and the doctor. Then she stepped toward me, her light shining in my face.

"Are you trying to leave us?" she asked.

"No," I said.

James muttered, "Why not? Why are you here anyway? Freakin' monster that makes no sense."

I stared at Tamra. "I will find one and bring it here."

The doctor said, "You can trust him, Tamra."

She shot him a dirty look but lowered her light from my face.

"Fine," she said. "We'll shut this door behind you. Doctor, I want you at the gate and watching. When he comes back, if he draws more than one, let us know. Adam, if you bring the horde, I'll shoot you in the head myself."

I said nothing.

She moved to the door and opened it just enough for me to slip out.

As I stepped out and the door shut behind me, I pressed up beside the wall and looked out at the concrete field where the zombies moved lazily about with nothing to draw their bloodlust.

―――――

It took me some time to get the attention of a zombie. Most of the ones I approached smelled me and moved away. But as I lingered among the group, after a while, they avoided me less. I became one of them again. Once they stopped avoiding me, I chose one at random.

I nudged it from behind, directing it toward the stadium.

It shuffled a couple of steps then turned to rejoin the group. I nudged it, carefully hitting it in the shoulder with my own, forcing it to stagger where I wanted it to go.

Dragging its feet, it took several staggering steps away from the group, then stopped. Its head swiveled toward the group. As it turned to shuffle back, I nudged it again, this time from the other side, blocking its view of the group.

It shuffled forward a few more steps. Then a few more.

I walked closely behind it. Shadowing it step for step. Every few steps nudging it with my shoulders, or pressing my chest against its back, pushing it forward just like a press of zombie bodies behind it would.

Finally, we reached the stadium and the door. The zombie stopped a few inches from the door. Its mouth opened and closed like a fish gasping for water.

I looked behind us. None of the others paid us any attention.

Carefully, I tapped on the glass of the door.

A piece of paper covering the window peeled back. Tamra stared out, seeing the zombie right in front of her. She looked past it and saw me pressed up against the zombie. She nodded at me and replaced the corner of the paper.

The door clicked loudly in the night's silence. I looked back toward the group. None heard it.

Slowly, the door opened inward.

I shuffled forward behind the zombie, encouraging it to take steps through the open space. It did. Slowly. It shuffled on the ground, across the doorsill, then across the laminate floor. I pressed up behind it until the door closed behind me.

Someone pressed a length of rope in my hand.

Before the zombie could react to the smell of fresh human meat in the room, I wrapped the rope tightly around its arms and looped it down around its feet.

As it fell to the floor, I moved to catch it, to dull any sound it might make.

It groaned and struggled against the bonds, trying to follow the scent to warm blood.

The room was dark. None of the others had flipped on their lights, but I saw them pressed up against the walls staring into the dark.

Tamra and the doctor stood with their heads cocked to the side, listening for what they could not see.

"You can use the lights now," I said.

James flipped his flashlight on first.

"Shit," he said in disbelief. "You did it. You caught one."

I peered down at the zombie I was restraining with my knee. It was a ragged one. The minimal remnants of clothing that had not been torn or rotted off revealed dead grey skin just as torn and ragged. Open gashes, an abdominal hole, a gaping cheek, and a missing eye revealed how horrific a change this one had gone through. The creature's stench in the small room was dreadful.

"Do you want it to stay in this room?" I asked.

Tamra shook her head.

"No," she said. "We need to move it to an upper floor where we can keep it away from people and where whatever noise it makes won't draw others."

I stood up and yanked the creature to its feet. James stepped out into the hall ahead of us to make sure there was no one to see what we were doing.

Once he nodded at me, I dragged the zombie behind me, up the sloping hall, to a set of stairs leading further up. While the zombie was not cooperating, it wasn't fighting me either. It simply preferred to keep trying to get at James, Tamra, and the doctor as they followed behind.

Finally, at the top of the stairs, I stepped aside so James could lead the way. He shined his flashlight along the landing and down the hall to the first door on that landing. He shoved the door open and stood to the side, allowing me to drag the zombie past him.

Once in the room, Tamra directed me to secure the zombie to the back of a chair that was clamped to the floor. Forcing it into a seated position on the floor was easy enough. I didn't have to worry about hurting it. It sat there, its back against the back of the chair, struggling to break the rope.

"Now what?" asked James.

The doctor stepped forward.

"Adam, can you keep it from biting me, and you, so I can get some samples? They will be my baseline before we begin testing my idea."

I sat next to the zombie. Looking around on the floor, I found a stick-like object. I shoved it between the zombie's teeth and held it, pressing it so hard it held the creature's head still against the chair.

"Okay, doctor," I said. "Is this good?"

He nodded at me and settled on the floor beside us before he started sorting out his instruments.

After a few minutes, he began taking the samples he wanted, while Tamra and James shined their lights on us, waiting for the next step of the doctor's plan.

———

Tamra and James left the room as daylight brightened outside the windows. James promised to return with some newspapers to tape over the windows so no one from below could see that we were keeping a zombie captive.

When I asked why it mattered, the doctor replied, "People will ask questions we don't have answers to. And when we, their leaders, don't have answers, they react with fear and distrust. No. It's better we keep this quiet for now. Just like the creature you are taking care of."

I wondered how the little thing was doing left alone. I didn't think it could move on its own yet, and like me, it didn't seem to feel a great need to feed. I had tried to go with James and Tamra so I could check on the creature, but all three insisted I stay with Dr. Odensea, if nothing else, to keep him safe from the zombie.

And so, I settled on the floor next to the putrid thing as it continued to squirm in its mindless desire to feed on the doctor.

The light increased, as did the warmth in the room. While I didn't feel the change in temperature much, I could tell the doctor did. Sweat beaded on his forehead and face and dripped off his nose. Scowling, he wiped his face.

"I'm going to ruin these samples, dammit," he murmured to himself.

I just watched him work.

After a while, he scooted away from the zombie. He tucked all the samples into his bag and looked at me.

Taking a deep breath, he pointed at the creature. "We might need another one of these," he said. "No. Actually. We will need another one of these. I need to try two methods to prove or disprove this idea I have about you. For now, I need you to do something."

I stared at him.

He continued, "I need you to let it bite you."

I still stared at him.

Taking my silence and my lack of movement to mean I was uncooperative, he leaned forward, resting his hands on his outstretched legs as he peered at me.

"Adam. I think you are contagious."

I said nothing.

He said, "I think when that zombie bit you, somehow you infected it. I think that creature in the ambulance results from your disease."

I looked at the zombie and said, "The other one didn't change."

Dr. Odensea cocked his head to the side as he said, "How could it? You tore its brains out. It never had a chance to respond to biting you. But the pathogen, or virus, or whatever is making you change might have spread to that zombified baby, changing it to be like you."

I looked back at the doctor. "You think I have a disease? What happens if this disease stops or is cured? Will I go back to being like that?"

The doctor shrugged. "I don't know. I do know that you did not turn back into a zombie after that other one bit you, so you are now immune to zombie attacks. If I can understand how, I might be able to create a vaccine for humans that would do the same. Make them immune, that is. Then again, it might make us turn into more of your kind, so I'm not ready to test that yet."

He shifted where he sat and tucked his legs under him. He leaned toward me and the zombie, a look of interest in his stare. Then he said, "I need you to let that thing bite you, Adam."

I nodded. Carefully, I removed the gag that was keeping the zombie from biting. While I did that, the doctor opened his notebook and started writing things in it.

As he wrote, I heard him murmur, "the date is... the time is... Adam is going to allow himself to be bitten by a zombie."

He looked up at me and nodded for me to continue.

I put my forearm up to the zombie's mouth. It chomped down, but then threw its head back as if in revulsion. With my other hand, I reached out and pushed the back of its head toward my waiting forearm, shoving it between its rotted teeth. I felt my skin break under the sharp teeth but registered no sensation of pain. For good measure, I shifted my arm a little and forced another bite right next to the first.

"Did that hurt you?" the doctor asked in a hushed voice.

"No. No pain," I said as I removed my arm and inspected the bites. The thick blueish purple fluid that filled me slowly oozed into the bites but did not truly bleed as a human or animal wound would have. I held it out to the doctor to examine.

He looked at the bites closely, writing notes as he did. Next, he set the notebook aside and pulled out swabs from his bag. He swabbed both wounds, labeled the samples, and replaced them in the bag.

"Okay. Thank you. Now, let's re-secure that thing. Then we should return to the ambulance. I have a lot to do."

I turned my attention to the zombie, noting that it was still. Its eyes, completely red even to the iris, were out of focus. It no longer struggled to get to the doctor. I said so, making the doctor pause and quickly reach into his notebook to jot down my observation.

After re-gagging the zombie, I stood up and stared down at it.

"Do you notice anything else I need to know?" Dr. Odensea asked.

"The smell. Is less," I said.

"Less? Less than what?" he asked.

"Less bad," I said.

I turned and left the room.

CHAPTER THIRTEEN

ON MY WALK back to the ambulance by the main gate, I couldn't help but notice the people appeared to be settling in.

The original crush of tents and bedrolls within the immediate area had been cleared out. Instead, bedrolls were moved into the hallways. Many had spaced out, even setting up small barriers, creating little walls for added privacy. Meanwhile, those who had tents were moving them out into the stadium, onto the softer soil. I stood at the edge of the dirt floor of the stadium and watched people working. They seemed to like this new place.

Looking around, I could see why. Now that the covers were pulled back, bright sunshine lit the entire field. Out in the middle, on a small rise, several people were talking, pointing at the ground, picking up the soil, and smelling it.

"They are thinking about planting a garden," Tamra said from beside me, as she, too, looked out at the small group.

"We are staying," I said.

"We are still waiting for Michael's group, and we don't know how long that will be. While we wait, we will try to make the best of where we are," she said in reply. "Once the others are here, they may like it here as well. We'll take a vote. If most people want to stay, then we will."

She fell silent, and I continued to watch the people as they scratched out lines in the dirt, creating large squares that I knew would be marked to grow specific things.

Tamra's presence beside me made me curious. I looked at her. Catching my movement out of the corner of her eye, she turned to face me.

"I just can't figure you out," she said plainly. "You help us. But I can't figure out why. You're not one of us. You're clearly not one of them. Dr. Odensea swears you are intelligent and have a sense of right and wrong, but he also says you are not human. So, Adam, tell me: why are you here?"

I stared into her green eyes, noting the golden flecks at the edges. Her posture and the smell of adrenaline building in her told me she was afraid of me and upset. Was she upset because she was afraid of me?

"I am here because of Michael. He did not kill me. He could have. I am here because of the doctor. He did not kill me. He could have. I am here because of you. You wanted to kill me. You did not. There is a part of me, the doctor thinks it is called genetic memory, which wants to be like you, and the doctor, and Michael. I want to be able to choose to allow something to live, because I can see beyond the thing that scares me."

Tamra bit her lip and looked away for a moment. She took a deep breath, her chest shuddering slightly, giving away a flood of emotions I didn't understand.

Finally, she looked back at me and said, "I get that."

She walked away, but after a couple steps, she turned back and said, "That, Adam, is more than just genetic memory. That makes humanity human."

―――――

Back in the ambulance, sitting with the tiny thing like me, I watched the doctor as he worked. Neither the small creature, for lack of a better way to describe it, nor I had any need to move about, so we simply sat still. It stared at me with its lifeless eyes, and I focused either on the doctor or on the space across from me.

As I sat, I thought of what Tamra had said. I wondered if, despite all the doctor's conclusions, I was not a bit human after all. Could non-human creatures exhibit human traits?

I thought of *Watership Down*. Certainly, the rabbits in the book seemed to, though the doctor had said repeatedly that in real life, rabbits had no such tendencies. And yet, I wondered. If other creatures, like cats and dogs—creatures that humans formed deep attachments to—could build bonds based on trust, loyalty, and gratitude, were they also showing signs of humanity?

Or was Tamra mistaken?

Was the evidence of those traits a sign of something more basic to life in general?

Could my display of those characteristics define life in me despite the lack of a heartbeat?

Was that why zombies could not share those qualities? Because they were dead walking?

I contemplated those ideas for hours, paying no attention to the doctor as he worked through the day.

Only when he finally felt a need to relieve himself did I shift my focus.

When he stepped out of the ambulance, I looked down at the tiny thing.

"Will you also exhibit signs of life?" I asked it.

Of course, it said nothing. It simply stared at me. I reached out a finger and touched the tip of its nose. Then I laid my hand next to it. At first, it did nothing, but then, quicker than I imagined it could move, it reached out and grabbed one of my fingers, wrapping its tiny hand around it tightly.

I found my face reacting without thinking. Looking up, staring at the polished metal doors of the storage cabinets there, I saw my first genuine smile.

At that moment, the back door opened, and the doctor stood staring up at me.

"Are you smiling?" he asked, a look of shock on his face.

I looked back at my hazy reflection. The smile fell away. My face once more a blank space, I looked back at the doctor and then down at the little thing.

"It is holding my finger," I said.

He quickly climbed in and shut the door behind him. Bending over the creature, he stared at it a moment before moving back to sit at his make-shift desk.

"That made you smile?" he asked me.

"Yes," I said simply.

The doctor nodded, gave me a small smile of his own, and added a note to his notebook.

He pointed at the creature and said, "It's time we take its measurements. Bring it here, please."

I did as asked. Like the first time, I helped with the measuring, making sure the little creature's mouth never got close to the doctor.

"It has no teeth; would its bite still be harmful?" I asked the doctor.

He stopped writing and looked up at me with a strange look on his face. Then he peered over the creature, staring into its mouth.

"I hadn't noticed. Of course, that makes sense, but I think it would still be harmful to a human. Teeth or not. Plenty of us have been bitten by zombies who had long ago lost their teeth because of the rot."

I said nothing in response. It was true. I had seen many zombies with barely any jaw or actual mouth left still wound and feed on a human.

Dr. Odensea added, "It is a good question though, Adam. A good question indeed."

He sat back on his stool and looked me over from head to toe.

"Tell me, after being bitten twice by that one we have upstairs, how do you feel? Are you experiencing any pain or noticing any changes?"

I took the little one and sat back down as I said, "No."

After placing it back in the container, I held out my arm for the doctor to see.

He leaned in to get a close look.

"The first one from its mother is entirely healed. Very good. Now, this one... This is the first bite from the one upstairs?" he asked.

"Yes," I said.

"It is already healing. Look how the edges are coming together. Interesting," he murmured.

He leaned closer to the second wound.

"This one is already healing, too. Though maybe because it is more ragged than the first, it appears to be closing more slowly." He reached behind him and grabbed a wooden stick he called a tongue depressor. He poked the second wound with it.

"Does that hurt at all?"

I said, "No."

He continued to poke at the wound, pulling back sections of ragged skin, then carefully placing it back. Satisfied that the zombie did not infect me, he threw away the depressor and sat up straight.

"I know I have said it before, but I will say it again: you are indeed a wonder, Adam."

He scooted his stool closer to his workspace and returned to looking at tissue samples.

"Was there any growth with the little one?" I asked him.

"Hmm?" he started, then, looking at me, he said, "Oh. No. No change since the first measurements. But we will keep checking every day. Now... I have work to do."

Realizing he was done talking, I looked back at the creature. Then, I leaned back against the side of the ambulance and simply waited.

Day passed to night. The doctor left me to sleep in a tent James had set up for him somewhere nearby. The tiny creature and I were silent and motionless.

In the deepest part of the night, I wondered about the zombie we left alone on the top floor. I left the ambulance. The camp was still. A man stood watch on a ladder that leaned up against the gate so he could see over the top. I knew another was at the other gate. But they were the only two still awake, and they were not concerned about anything within the stadium, only outside it.

As I observed the man on the ladder, I listened for sounds of the zombies out there. I heard the shuffle of their feet. Listless. Aimless. A dry crunch of leather or rubber or bare bones dragging against the dirt collected on the concrete field. Nothing alarming except the fact that they were still there.

I listened a moment longer, then moved into the hallway and made my way up to the room on the top level.

On entering the room, I startled Tamra. With the door open behind me, I saw her blink in my direction as she struggled to turn on her flashlight.

"It's me. Adam," I said.

She relaxed but still turned on the light.

"What time is it?" she asked, her voice deep and husky from sleep.

"I don't know," I said. "Everyone else is still asleep."

She pointed the light at the zombie, who was now struggling against its bonds.

"Why are you here?" she asked me as she watched the zombie.

"I told you..." I started to answer.

"No. No. Why are you here in this room in the middle of the night?" she asked impatiently.

"I was wondering if there were any changes," I said simply.

She looked at me, before looking back at it.

"None that I can tell," she said. "It still wants to eat me, I think. It is only still when I go completely still. But when I twitch even a little, it goes a little crazy trying to break those bonds."

I closed the door behind me and sat on the floor by the door, my back to the wall.

"You think the doctor is right?" I asked Tamra, "about me?"

Tamra shrugged. "He seems pretty insistent that you could be an answer, some sort of savior for humanity."

I watched her in silence. She paused and rubbed her temples, before she continued, "I don't know what to think beyond the fact that you are dangerous. And if there are more of you, or will be more of you, I want to know."

She looked me in the eye, "and if you are as dangerous as I think you are, I want to know how to kill you."

She watched me, waiting for me to respond, I suppose, but I had nothing to say about that.

Instead, I looked back at the zombie and said, "I don't sense any changes either. Other than it doesn't smell as bad as it did when I brought it in."

She looked back at it. Cocking her head back, she took in a long breath through her nose. She glanced back at me.

"It still stinks pretty bad," she said.

"It does," I agreed, "But it was worse."

Tamra lay back down on her bedroll. Facing the ceiling, she flipped off her flashlight. I watched her settle in, trying to ease the tension in her shoulders, back, and arms.

After a moment, she spoke into the dark, "If you intend on staying, monitor that thing, will you?"

"I will," I said, and she closed her eyes. I sensed her fall asleep within minutes, leaving me alone to stare at the rotting corpse across from me.

CHAPTER FOURTEEN

THE DOCTOR KEPT TALLY marks on the wall of ambulance to record the passing of days. Glancing at them, I knew we'd spent a week in the stadium before the doctor had me go out and bring another zombie in the middle of the night. At that point, some of the other people knew about the first, though none knew of the little creature I was watching over.

Tamra had explained to those people why we had a zombie captive, and why we were getting another. I think she was hoping some of them would offer to keep watch over them. When none of them did, she tasked a couple so she could get some actual restful sleep in a place not shared with a thing that wanted to rip her apart.

Once I got the second zombie up to the room, James helped me secure it to another chair, just like the first one. Once it was tied up, the doctor sat next to it and began readying his tools for the samples he wanted to take.

"Okay, Adam. Just like last time, please keep it from biting me," he said.

I did as he asked. He got his samples. When he was finished, he leaned away from the zombie and looked at me.

"Okay. I need you to do something different this time, Adam."

I waited for him to continue. He seemed hesitant. Shifting things around in his bag, not looking at me, he said, "I need you to bite it."

He looked at me. I could see he was serious. And he clearly disliked asking me to do this. I looked at the zombie. Its mouth was not yet gagged, and it strained wildly against the rope that held it in place. The fibers of the rope rustled and whispered as the zombie exerted all its weight.

I stared at the creature a moment, then reverted my gaze to the doctor.

"You want me to bite it? Where?"

The doctor looked surprised. Clearly, he hadn't thought about it.

"Well, it does not have a working circulatory system, so biting it in the wrist isn't likely to get a good result. Though that should mean it won't matter where you bite it at all."

I looked back at the dead thing. Disgust filled me. Bite it? Overcome with a powerful revulsion, I nearly got up and walked out of the room. Yet, I stayed where I was and stared at the creature.

Finally, without waiting for the doctor to decide, I snapped my head toward the zombie and sank my teeth into its neck.

Once. Quick. Just a bite. I broke its thin skin, but didn't bite hard enough to remove any of its rotting flesh.

Still, as I jerked away from it, the taste of it lingered in my mouth and I felt a sudden desire to rip out my tongue. It was death. Rot. Disease. Rage. Bitterness. All in that one bite. I felt my face shift in reaction.

"Gross?" the doctor asked me as he studied my face. "You look like a human after sucking on a lemon."

I shook my head and closed my eyes, wishing I could think of a way to get the taste out of my mouth.

"Never again," I said to Dr. Odensea. "I will not bite another one."

I opened my eyes and saw the doctor nodding at me.

He said, "Just this one, Adam. Thank you. I will not ask you to do that again."

He pulled more stuff out of his bag. After he took more samples, he started to leave.

Pausing by the door, looking at the first zombie, he directed his attention to James.

"See to it that one is killed and removed from here. Its tests were all negative. Biting Adam had no effect on it," he said as he left the room.

James pulled a knife from his belt and approached the zombie.

I got up and raised a hand.

"Let me," I told him.

James looked at me, skepticism edged into his face, but after a moment, he seemed to change his mind.

He handed me his blade and stepped back to watch.

I held the blade in one hand. Never having held one before, I looked at it, turning it from side to side, testing my grip on the leather-wrapped handle.

I approached the first zombie and knelt in front of it. It couldn't hurt me. It was a monster. Everything about it revolted me. Especially now after having bitten the other one. It was a dead thing that needed to be truly and completely dead.

And yet...

Part of me felt a strange hesitation.

I was once this thing. Part of me was still like it. I was different, but the rage and the hunger that had driven me was still there. It was just a much smaller part of me. More like a bad memory.

Knowing the creature had to go, I lifted the blade and slammed it down into its skull. All the way to the hilt.

Immediately, the zombie went still.

I pulled the blade out and straightened up.

Without saying a word, I handed the knife back to James and left him standing there with the other zombie straining to get at him.

———

I entered the ambulance and closed the door firmly behind me. As I turned toward the interior, the expression on the doctor's face froze me in place.

In his gloved hands, he held the tiny creature.

"Adam," he said, his voice low and trembling, "This..."

He held the creature out to me. I looked at it. The slight flutter in my mind when I saw it was still alive had me grip the bench that I normally sat on. I looked back at the doctor as he continued, "This creature is growing."

I stayed where I was. The terror and uncertainty in the doctor's voice, in his very posture, and in the aroma coming off him worried me.

He still had the creature extended toward me, and he nodded at me.

"I won't harm it, Adam. I promised you I would not. Please, take it." The pleading in his voice, and the remembered promise, made the fluttering in my mind dissipate.

Reaching out, I took the tiny thing from Dr. Odensea and resumed my normal seat, with the creature lying in my lap.

"It is growing," I repeated.

The doctor leaned against his work area and pointed at a screen showing various images and things he called graphs.

"Yes. It weighs a bit more, despite not consuming anything. Its head is a centimeter bigger, and its body is three centimeters longer. I also measured its arms, legs, and girth—that is around its stomach," he said, and paused before speaking again. "Did you notice this creature has no reproductive parts?"

I stared at him. Confused.

He leaned back and stared back at me, a shocked expression on his face.

"You, as a previous human, have healed over reproductive parts of your body. I had not thought about it, though I guess I should have. Zombies procreate through their bites, so they do not procreate the way humans do. I assumed as you change into whatever you are still becoming, that you would regain the desire and ability to procreate as humans do. But," he pointed at the creature lying still on my legs, "that one has neither male nor female reproductive parts. With your permission, I'd like to do an ultrasound of it, to see whether its internal body has those organs or not."

He stopped and looked at me. "I'd also like to re-evaluate you and see if you are still changing internally and externally."

Reproduction. Procreation. The concepts were not new to me. In the books the doctor and Michael had shared with me, the concepts were hinted at if not outright illustrated. I was curious about the concepts but had no real feeling one way or the other about them.

Seeing that he was waiting for my consent, I handed the creature back to him.

"No," he replied. "It is better you hold it while I do the ultrasound. I can bring the machine closer to you. You can hold it and turn it as I need you to."

He flipped the device on and scooted his stool closer to me and the creature. He squeezed some gooey stuff onto its stomach. I watched the creature as it focused first on the doctor, then on the machine the doctor held before it.

As soon as the device touched the creature, the screen showed fuzzy images that made no sense to me. As the doctor manipulated the apparatus over the creature's stomach, the images shifted and changed. The doctor muttered as he moved it ever so slowly, recording each move. He went back over it taking more measurements and zooming in for more clear imagery.

Finally, he finished.

After he carefully cleaned the goo off the creature, he scooted back to his workspace. There, he stared at the images for a moment before turning to me. Once again, he seemed overcome with amazement.

"The creature has no reproductive organs, Adam."

I asked him, "What does that mean?"

He shrugged and said, "I don't know exactly, but let me use a fairy tale creature to illustrate what I think it means. Some scary stories humans used to tell were of a human species that had evolved into something immortal. These creatures were no longer human. They were what humans called vampires. They did not reproduce like humans, but if they bit a human, that human could change to become a vampire. Because of this different sort of reproduction, they were rumored to be few. Speculation in the stories was that they were few because they were immortal—that they self-regulated because they relied on the human population to feed them. Other speculation was that because they were immortal, they had no desire to reproduce, and that the few times when they changed a human into one of them, it was either an accident, or extremely deliberate."

I stared at the doctor. I was familiar with the stories of vampires, werewolves, mummies, and even zombies. Humans thought all those creatures were fake. Until zombies took over.

"I am a vampire?" I asked, confused.

Dr. Odensea laughed. After a moment, he stopped and grew serious once more.

"No. Not a vampire, but the more you change, the more I think there was some element of truth to those old tales. Without destroying your brain, I think you are nearly indestructible. I can cut you. But you regenerate. The tests I did on you and your brain should have harmed you but clearly, they did not. For all I know, you could be immortal. On the other hand, that one on your lap is growing, and therefore aging, but slower than a human baby would. This could mean that you, too, are aging, but at a much slower rate than I would. This means you could live several human lifetimes, or that you simply keep aging and regenerating, and… Be immortal."

He grew silent. I looked down at the creature. Trying to process what he was saying, I realized I was also a little irked.

"We need a name. Undone," I said.

The doctor looked at me. He said nothing at first, but then he nodded as he commented, "Fitting. I like it."

Then I pointed to the little one and said, "We need to name it, too," I said.

"Of course. Yes," responded the doctor.

He leaned toward me and stared at the creature for a moment, then he sat back and returned his attention to the scans.

"You name it, Adam. Later, I will do some ultrasounds on you as well, okay?"

I looked down at the creature.

I thought of the human names I knew.

Michael. Cal. Tamra. James.

I thought of the names of people and creatures in the books I had read.

Alice. Hazel. Zeus. Winnie. Bambi. Mary. George.

None of those seemed right for this tiny thing.

I stared into its eyes. There was intelligence there. While it was not yet able to communicate, it was there. I wondered what it would like to be called.

I talked to it while the doctor worked.

"What name would be good for you?" I asked.

It just stared at me.

I closed my eyes and thought. As I sat there with my eyes closed, I recalled wandering with the zombies as I first realized I was changing. I remember looking upward into the great expanse that stretched above us during the day. First recollections of feelings beyond hunger and rage. The blue sky stretching ever upward, ever outward. No matter how far we walked, or how far I ambled when I left the horde, the sky still stretched out above me.

I opened my eyes, looked at the creature and saw in it a prospect of the future running ever before me.

"Sky," I said to it.

I looked at Dr. Odensea and said, "This one will be called Sky."

The doctor looked up at me first, and at the tiny creature next.

He nodded once and said, "So be it. Hello, little Sky."

Then he turned back to his work.

CHAPTER FIFTEEN

SHOUTS from outside the ambulance made me put Sky down. I knew it would not go anywhere. I opened the back of the vehicle and stepped out into the night. The shouting came from the gate.

I ran to see a small group already gathered.

Tamra, at the foot of the ladder, yelled up to the guard, "Are you certain it's Michael?"

The man called back down, "He gave the signal. Looks like it is his group. A few vehicles short, but they are coming fast!"

Tamra waved him off the ladder.

"Okay, everyone, listen up! Get this gate open. Let the vehicles in and keep the zombies out!"

She turned to James, who'd just run up behind me.

"James, get that ambulance out of the way! Now!" she shouted. She looked at me and said, "You. I want you to help keep the monsters out. Got it?"

I rushed forward just as the humans pulled the heavy bracing bar from its rack. I helped prop it up to one side and as the gate cracked open, I stepped outside into the beams of light coming from the speeding vehicles.

Somewhere behind me, I heard a radio crack to life.

Michael's disembodied voice called out, "Tamra, that you? God, I hope it is. We have been running for days. Almost out of fuel. Horde is two clicks behind us. We need to get inside. Then we need to run."

I turned to Tamra, who was holding the walkie talkie thing in her hands, a frozen look on her face. Holding my gaze, she clicked a button and spoke into the device.

"It's Tamra. Good you're finally here, man. Just get your people inside. We'll discuss once you are safely in."

The walkie crackled in her hand.

"Get your people ready to run, Tam. I mean it."

The walkie went silent.

I turned just as the first vehicle rushed past me and into the stadium.

Just as it moved past, the zombies from the concrete field got close enough to be a threat. Responding to the noise of the gate, the vehicles, and the walkie, they moved as one toward the gate.

I stepped toward one and shoved it backward into several behind it. They all fell to the ground in a heap but were soon replaced by another few. I killed one. Then two. Then three.

Another vehicle zoomed by, the wind of its passing distracting me as another zombie tried to get past it. I flung out an arm. Instinctively, the zombie bit into it. Letting it clamp on, I swung my arm, turning my whole body with it. I chucked the creature into others, knocking more of them down.

Another vehicle rushed past me. Then another.

Behind me, I heard people from my group fighting the zombies.

I looked out in the direction the vehicles had been coming from. Three more.

Someone behind me screamed in agony. As I turned, I saw one of the young men fall under the weight of several zombies. I rushed to get them off. The young man fought, killing one, and pushing another away, leaving just one more.

I yanked it off him, slammed my fist down on its skull, crushing into its brain, effectively killing it.

I helped the man to his feet.

He glanced over his arms and legs.

"Am I bit?" he screamed. "Am I bit?"

I leaned toward him, inhaling deeply.

"No. Keep fighting," I told him.

He looked at me for a moment. I could see the battle with terror in his eyes, but his courage seemed to win. He nodded and turned to stop another few zombies from reaching the gates as two more vehicles moved through the gate.

Finally, the last vehicle approached. As it reached me, it slowed down. Michael sat at the wheel. He looked at me. His expression was one of deep sadness, but also a glimmer of relief.

He waved and gave me a fragile smile. The next moment, he was past me and in the stadium.

Behind me, Tamra whistled. The signal to return.

I waited until the humans were all safely back in. The gate was nearly shut. I killed another three zombies before I slipped into the stadium and the gate was secured.

I turned around and immediately found myself wrapped in human arms. I stood still. Frozen.

"Adam!" Michael exclaimed, squeezing me before he stepped back.

"I think you have gotten taller," he said, appraising me from head to toe. "It' so good to see you. I was worried..." his voice trailed off. He turned to Tamra, "Thank you for not..." he glanced at me sideways, then said to her, "you know."

Tamra frowned, but she said, "It turned out to be quite useful."

She gave me a sharp nod and looked back at Michael. "Now, tell me, why do you think we need to run? This is a rather good set-up. Why don't you have your group settle in, get recovered. Then we can talk about what happened to you all out there."

Michael shook his head.

"No. Tamra. You don't understand. The horde that hit the settlement. It found us. It followed us. I mean. I am certain it tracked us."

"Impossible," said Tamra. "You clearly need some rest. Come on. Not another word. Not now. Get fed. Get sleep. It's a few hours till sunup. Then, you can tell us more."

She didn't let him argue with her, but I could smell his distress. He was truly afraid.

I looked at Michael while I listened to the remaining zombies outside the wall. Their numbers were less now, but they were enough to be a threat to the people here. If a horde was coming, the gate, even with its considerable bracing would not be enough to stop the press of bodies against it.

But Tamra was the boss here, and she clearly still did not trust me.

I watched her lead Michael into the stadium. Then, I noted that his group had circled their vehicles just inside the gate all pointed back toward it.

They were ready to run.

———

I sat on one side of Michael while his wife sat on the other side of him. They were lost in private conversation, so I focused my attention on the others from their group. Michael said they had left with four dozen people. Sitting around the fires now were only twenty.

They all smelled of terror. When they first arrived, they were tense and on edge. Most were still anxious, but nearly all of them were trying hard to relax. In that relaxation, they revealed their exhaustion. Most could barely keep their eyes open and were clearly fighting to stay awake enough to eat and drink.

I'd overheard one of the young women say the adults hadn't eaten in days. They fed the young on the run, eating from cut open rations, or eating unmixed MREs right out of the packaging. As she spoke, some children held back gagging reflexes, but I could tell they had been the focus of care among the group.

Tamra and Dr. Odensea approached, casting sidelong glances at the group.

"Can we join you?" the doctor asked Michael.

Michael nodded.

Tamra and the doctor sat on the ground across from Michael and his wife. They both looked around the group, appraising. Counting. Confusion and concern on their faces.

"What happened?" Tamra finally asked.

We all looked at Michael.

He took a deep breath, and a drink of water, before he started.

"I will not go into heavy detail. Okay? We lost too many. And the journey was never ending. We were harassed the entire time. The longest spot of rest we could get was maybe a day. But that was right after leaving the settlement. That was before the horde found us."

Dr. Odensea interrupted, "You said the horde tracked you. That is impossible. Surely you know that."

Michael glared at the doctor. "Impossible? Really, doc? When we have the impossible slowly eating away at the human population every day? When you have another impossible thing sitting right here among us?" He looked at me. "I don't mean that negatively, Adam, but it is true." He returned his attention to the doctor.

"Let me tell you what happened. Okay? But I will begin by saying this: I estimate we have maybe six hours before the horde arrives. Maybe."

Michael looked at his wife. She gave him an encouraging nod while she fidgeted with a gold band on her finger.

He said, "As I was saying, we had a day of decent rest after we left the settlement. As we were heading east, we ran into several roadblocks and had to find ways around them. This took time, each time. Trying to get the back vehicles turned around, deciding on another route. You know how it goes when we have to caravan.

"Thing is, some roadblocks were new. I'd just been down some of those roads when we had gone out foraging. But there were no people waiting to attack. The roads were just blocked. Downed trees, debris, nothing too big, or too heavy, just a lot. To clear the roads would've taken too long and made too much noise. So, we diverted. Again, and again. Three days after leaving the settlement, I sent three guys to go back and make sure everyone got out okay. While we waited, that was the full day, we were gathered around an old gas station that sat near a river. Everyone was tired, but we were all in good spirits. As much as can be expected after being forced to run." He paused and took another sip of water.

Michael looked up at the sky and continued, "Late that night, one of the three returned. He was bit, wounded, and terrified. He confirmed the settlement was clear. They found the second caravan's tracks heading out. Then they found the horde had followed the tracks. The guys decided to follow the horde for a bit to see if it continued after you all, or if they would divert as they often do for something else. They'd followed along behind, thought they were keeping quiet, and stayed well enough behind that they lost sight of the horde through trees or over hilltops. At one such hill, when they crested it, the horde was gone."

Michael bowed his head, sadness and disbelief edging his voice. "They went down the hill to see if they could follow the horde just to be sure it was no longer following the caravan. He said they got about halfway down the hill when the zombies moved out from the edges of the forest as though they had been waiting. They moved as though they had been signaled. Instead of moving away from the men I sent, the horde turned on them. The men ran back up the hill, but two fell. The one who made it back to us fought to break through the zombies. He ran back to the settlement, and then he came to us. He died an hour later, and we made sure he didn't change. Two hours after that, the horde appeared."

Michael stopped for a moment. He just stared into the fire. I looked at the fire, too. What was he seeing in the flames? I watched the flames shift and dance on the breeze. Sparks swirled high into the air.

When Michael resumed, his voice was low, barely above a whisper. While he spoke, I continued to stare into the flames, dread settling in my mind.

"The zombies attacked, and we ran. At first, we just piled in, didn't even try to fight them. Having lost the three I had sent back to the settlement, I wasn't ready to lose any more. So, I directed the group to get to the next point on the map that I had shown the drivers earlier in the day. I'm glad I did rather than hoping they could all just follow along as they had before. We got separated immediately. I led in the first vehicle, but watched one forced to veer off on a side road. Several at the back were forced to go back the way we had come from. From that point on, we lost vehicles. And from that point on, we were followed by the horde. We should have put great distance between us and the horde, but every time we stopped to rest, we'd barely get camp set up when we'd be alerted to their presence. And a couple times they got up close, and we lost more people."

Tamra leaned in and scowled at him.

"There are a lot of zombies in the world. We can't go anywhere without running into them anymore. Yet you seem pretty convinced it was the exact group that attacked the settlement. Is that right?" she asked.

Michael's wife leaned forward and said, "It was. And we know it was..."

"But how can you know for sure?" Tamra asked as she tapped a foot impatiently.

"Because some of ours were among the walking dead!" Michael snapped. "Some of us were there in each attack. Old Sam. Janice. Ricky. Manuel. Heidi. Our people! Every time!"

Tamra sat back, her shoulders slumped, disbelief still on her face, but also shock. I too felt a sense of loss. Old Sam was the woman I'd met so briefly helping her into the vehicle. I had been looking forward to seeing her again. Her fearlessness around me had made me like her instantly.

Dr. Odensea looked around at the others. "This is true?"

I watched as the others nodded, the scent of fear coming off them all.

One woman said quietly, "It was as though they were haunting us. Like ghosts. Zombies, of course, but we couldn't seem to leave them behind."

Michael leaned in and said to Tamra, "James told me you all witnessed some strange things as well."

Tamra and the doctor looked at me. Before they could respond, Michael continued, "Like the zombies' attack at the settlement. James told me you learned that the zombies did not feed like normal. Is that true?"

The doctor nodded. "It seems to be what everyone witnessed."

Michael looked at his wife. They both stood up and looked at everyone around them.

"We really need to be packing up and going. Like. Right. Now," he said.

Just then, a woman ran up, waving excitedly.

"There is a horde coming to the other gate. I think I saw Old Sam among them!"

CHAPTER SIXTEEN

WE ALL STOOD on the top floor of the stadium in one of the few rooms that had windows looking out and away from the structure.

With the sun rising in the east, it was easy to see the horde moving through the area to the east and south. I didn't know any of the ones that were lost to the horde at the settlement, but Michael, James, and Tamra recognized quite a few. Their astonishment revealed in their collective silence and wide eyes. The smell of fear filled the air.

As they discussed the impossibility of what was happening, Dr. Odensea was back in another room, trying to see if the captured zombie displayed any changes. I had wanted to tell Michael about it, but with the impending attack, the doctor told me it wasn't the right time.

So, I said nothing.

I just stood there, watching the horde. A writhing mass of undead surging forward, one shuffled step at a time. The sound of their approach was like a swarm of wasps on the wind. Before long, the stench of the horde overwhelmed my senses. This horde was several times the size of the one I had been part of.

Beside me, Tamra whispered, "God help us."

Michael left the room. I followed him as he rushed around to a similar room on the other side of the top level. He stared out over the open fields on that side of the stadium. I followed his gaze, and when he sagged with disappointment, I felt what he must be feeling.

The horde had surrounded the stadium. There was no way out for us. Not without sacrificing a lot of humans.

He looked at me, true fear in his eyes.

"This will be the end for us, Adam. But not for you. I think you can get through that. You can do that, can't you?"

At that moment, a new feeling overwhelmed me. How was he more worried about me right now? It made no sense. But there he was, showing genuine concern for me, a non-human, a non-zombie, something strange and scary. Even though most of the others were still afraid of me and certainly didn't trust me, he cared more about me than about his own life.

"I will stay," I said to him.

He sagged even more, bracing himself on the windowsill.

"We had come so far. We lasted for so long. To go out now..." his voice trailed off. I saw a drop of water slide down his cheek. Averting my stare, I watched the horde slowly amble toward the stadium.

Doom and death were coming.

Slow and steady.

Angry and hungry.

The sheer mass spread out below us was alarming, even to me. Was there nothing I could do to help the humans survive this?

As I stared out over the horde, I desperately tried to find a way I could help clear a path so they could escape. Escape was the only way. They could not fight off a mass this large. Not with their limited numbers.

Something caught my eye.

I stared at it. It was still too far away to be sure, but I watched it closely.

It moved closer, walking among the horde, though some zombies seemed to want to avoid it.

Closer.

Closer.

Then it stopped. It looked around. Then it looked up. With the horde moving around it and past it, it looked up, and it looked at me.

It made eye contact with me.

It was me.

It was another undone.

And the glare in its violet eyes was a promise of death.

Immediately, I pointed at it.

"Michael. Look," I said.

He stepped closer to my side and gazed in the direction I was pointing.

"What am I looking for?" he asked.

"One like me. See? There. Near the back of the horde now. It is moving slower than the others. It's looking right at us."

Michael squinted against the daylight and raised a hand to shield his eyes. Slowly, his jaw dropped. He looked at me, then back at it.

"Is that how the horde has been following us? Another one of you? And clearly just as intelligent?" he asked.

Standing so close to me, I heard his heart pounding in his chest. It was racing. I looked at him. His face was flushed. He paled and sweat beaded on his forehead. His eyes were wide as he stared at the creature that looked like me, with its strange eyes and blue skin.

"I don't know," I said in a low voice.

Michael turned away from the window and dashed out of the room, calling over his shoulder, "I need to tell the others."

Just outside the door, he stopped. Incredibly still, he looked back at me.

"Adam, I'm sorry. When I tell them my suspicions about the horde being led by one of you, things may change a lot around here. For you."

I stared at him. I knew what he meant. If the people saw that creature out there as a threat, their fears about me might take over. I imagined they would want to kill me.

Maybe Michael and the doctor could speak for me. Allow me to live but let me leave. Hopefully with Sky.

Thinking of Sky, I glanced back out at the other creature as it kept staring at me. I could not abandon it. Would the humans demand that of me? Could Sky and I survive on our own out in the wild? That creature seemed to be doing fine, though I could not fathom what it must be thinking leading the horde as it appeared to be doing.

I heard Michael breathing heavily behind me. Turning to him, I said, "The humans will do what they think is best. If they no longer trust me to be here, I will go. Please do not let them end me. Or Sky."

He started to walk away, then stopped again. "Sky? Who is Sky?"

I turned away from the windows and stepped toward Michael, my voice low, not wanting any of the others to overhear.

I said, "A small one of me. The doctor thinks I created it. By accident, but he is running all kinds of tests thinking I created it."

Michael paled even more. He reached out and braced himself on the doorframe.

"You made another one. I want to see it."

I said nothing. Michael was my first human friend. I trusted him. So, I silently led him down to where the ambulance was parked. Everyone else was busy setting up defenses and packing belongings. Nobody paid us any attention as I opened the back of the ambulance and let Michael climb up ahead of me.

He looked around the tight interior until I closed the door behind me. I pointed to the doctor's little stool. Michael sat down and watched me as I reached under the bench and pulled out the shallow metal tray that Sky lay in.

I set the tray on the bench and held Sky. Carefully, I held it under its arms so Michael could see it clearly.

He just stared. At Sky. At me. Then back at Sky.

Sky squirmed in my hands, so I shifted it into a cradled position and glanced down at it. It stared up at me, then turned its head to look at Michael.

He still just stared.

"This is Sky. Its human-turned-zombie mother was upstairs, tied to a chair. It bit me, and I killed it. Later, after Tamra led the people in here, someone was going to remove the zombie's body and saw Sky in the gaping cavity within it. I have been protecting it. Only James, who found it, Tamra, the doctor, and I know about Sky. And now you."

Michael tore his gaze from Sky and stared at me. His mouth made a strange shape. He started to say something, clamped his mouth shut, and started to say something again.

"Do you want to hold it?" I asked him.

His eyes shot open wide. He jerked backward away from me, shaking his head. I sank to the bench and laid Sky on my upper legs.

"I don't believe it will hurt you," I said, fighting my disappointment in Michael's reaction.

Michael shook his head and said, "Adam, how can you know?"

"I don't," I replied simply.

He leaned toward me, the color slowly returning to his face.

"I'm just trying to process what that little thing could mean for you and for us. I'm glad you all kept it a secret from the others. They would lose their minds! And my group... they'd demand we kill you both immediately. And now... With that other one out there... Oh god. Adam, this is terrible. Bad for us. Bad for you. Bad for that." He pointed at Sky.

He stared at Sky for a moment, then he looked at me.

"Adam, you must leave here. You can't worry about us. You can't stay to fight with us. Take Sky and find a place for you both to live away from humans."

I stared at him.

"No," I said.

"No?" he repeated back to me. "Don't you understand the danger you are both in? Especially now with that other one out there?"

I nodded as I had seen so many humans do when they were saying yes without saying the word.

"I understand. But you are my friend. And Dr. Odensea is a sort of friend. I like what I am learning from you humans and want to learn more. I can't do that when I am out there on my own. And I cannot teach Sky on my own. Sky will need to learn from humans. I don't know that it will have memories of what it was like to be human before the zombie change."

Michael sat back. I could tell he was considering my words. After a moment, he got up and squeezed between me and the gear on the other side of the ambulance. Hand on the door, he looked at me, then at Sky.

"I need to tell the others about what we saw out there. That will shape how they decide to react to this attack. I will tell them you are the one who saw it and alerted me. That may make a difference. Stay here. Stay quiet. If I think they are going to come for you, I will come get you first. I don't want them to kill you, Adam. Nor Sky. Okay?"

I stared at Michael. I could sense his determination. He wanted to save the humans. And he wanted to save me and Sky.

"Okay," I said. "I will stay here. For now."

He nodded and left.

CHAPTER SEVENTEEN

I WAITED in the ambulance for a while before someone came pounding on the back door.

"Adam!" the doctor called from outside the vehicle. "We need you!"

I hesitated, but he pounded on the door some more.

Carefully, I laid Sky back on the metal tray and hid it under the bench. I unlocked and opened the door.

I got out and closed the door behind me. When I turned to face the doctor, I noticed how disheveled he was. His hair a mess. Clothes unkempt. His eyes were wild.

"Michael told us about the other one out there like you. We went up to see for ourselves. I watched it for a while. The others went to fortify the gates. Running is not an option. We just don't have the numbers."

He paused to catch his breath.

"Can you hear them, Adam?"

"Yes," I said.

I had been hearing them for hours. The horde was all around the stadium. I heard the press of their broken bodies against the gates, along the walls. At first, it was just the crunch of their bodies. But just before the doctor knocked on the ambulance, I heard the cracking and the low creaking of the weight pressing inward against the gates. I knew they'd hold for a while. Several hours. Even a day. But other areas were weaker. The door that I had entered upon arriving, and at least two others like it. These would not hold back the wave of zombies insistent on getting in.

The doctor continued, "Is there anything you can do to help?"

I smelled the desperation in his sweat. He smelled just like Michael and his group did when they arrived.

True terror.

Right that moment, I heard the splinter of wood and glass from four different directions around the stadium; they seemed to be breached simultaneously, though I wasn't sure how that could be possible. The doctor turned to the closest sound of infiltration, his face white, his body trembling.

"Get the people onto the ramps. Have them fight on the ramps, and retreat backward," I said to the doctor.

He stared at me.

"Adam, there are too many. We'll never survive. And there is nowhere to go from those ramps. Just up until we are trapped."

I listened to the horde shifting and moving. They were still pressing on the main gates, but many were already flooding into the breaches where the regular doors had given way. Their stench filled the air. Shouts of the humans rose from every corner.

Michael and James ran up to me. The expression on James' face was angry and fierce. He was ready to kill.

"You!" he screamed in my face. "You did this."

I said nothing as Michael got in between us.

"Adam did not."

James squared up against Michael. "Why are you protecting this monster?"

He shoved Michael backward. I stepped up and stared down at James, who was a head shorter than me.

"Your fight is not with Michael. Your fight is with the zombies. I will fight with you."

James glared at me.

"What good are you? You can't kill all these creatures! You can't save us!" he shouted at me.

Tamra came running up shouting at James, "Enough, James! Do what I told you! Block the halls with the vehicles. Make the zombies work to get to us! Buy us time."

James glared at me some more, blade in his hand, the desire to press it into my skull clear on his face. I held his glare and said nothing.

Tamra shoved him, forcing him off balance as she screamed at him, "James! Now!"

He gritted his teeth and moved off to one of the trucks.

Tamra faced Michael. "You get that ambulance moved. Put it at the front of the line by the gate, then use every other vehicle you can to block the other ramp."

He nodded and turned to do as she asked.

Tamra watched him go before she turned to me.

"If you really want to help us, you better get moving."

The doctor spoke up at that point, "Adam suggested we move up the ramps…"

Tamra nodded, "Yes. That is what we are going to do. And we will lose, but we will die fighting."

James' words still rang in my mind. He was right. I couldn't kill all the zombies. I couldn't save these people to whom I'd formed some sort of attachment. But…

An idea popped into my mind.

I looked at Tamra first, and at the doctor next.

"I have an idea," I said to them.

Tamra cocked her head to the side. "Tell me."

I shook my head.

"I am still trying to sort it out," I told her.

The doctor stepped up and stared at me.

"You are going out there," he said simply.

Thinking hard, trying to envision what I had in mind, not knowing if it would work, I said, "I think I can make them all stop."

Tamra pressed past the doctor and stared up at me, her face streaked with dirt and sweat, her attention entirely on me despite the sounds of fighting all around us.

"How?" she asked simply.

I looked at the doctor, then back at her, trying to find the words that matched what I was envisioning in my mind. Finally, I said, "I am uncertain. But I think I can try."

Tamra threw her hands up in the air.

"Just great. The one thing we might have going for us in here, and you want to go out there to try something that may not work, and you don't even know what that something is. Just great."

She stormed off, yelling at people to move vehicles or get up the ramps.

The doctor stepped up to me, still trembling with fear.

"Are you leaving Sky?" he asked.

I turned to look at the ambulance where Sky was safely hidden. I knew the humans wouldn't find it. Only Michael and the doctor knew where it was hidden. And I doubted the zombies would breach the ambulance, meaning they wouldn't find it, and they wouldn't care if they did. Sky was safe.

"Yes."

The doctor bowed his head and took a shuddering breath. He glanced about the stadium as people rushed past us to get to the ramps before they were completely blocked.

I reached out and pushed him gently toward the closest one.

"Go. Live," I told him. "If I do not return, please keep Sky safe. Please keep looking for answers about us."

He blinked. Were those tears?

"And please tell Michael I said thank you for being my friend."

Without waiting for the doctor to respond, I moved toward the closest breach.

———

Leaving the humans behind, I approached the door that led to a room filling with zombies. It was the second room I had entered that first time I explored the stadium. I slipped into the room carefully. Initially, the zombies reacted to the flood of light, but not sensing a human, they resumed their steady press inward. One by one, I killed them all. I stacked their bodies next to the door I had just entered, hoping that would hold the breach for a while. But the press of zombies continued to pour into room.

Knowing I had to get out of the stadium to do what I hoped might stop the attack, I closed the other door and finished killing the zombies that had come in while I was stacking corpses. Leaving them scattered about the room, I slipped into the room that was open to the outside world. Again, I killed and stacked corpses against the interior door.

One. Two. Ten. Twenty.

The bodies piled up between me and the interior door. Still more zombies pressed in.

I could do no more to help stop that breach, so I worked my way through the sea of zombies, killing as I went.

Kill a zombie. Take a step. Kill another zombie. Take another step.

Their rage was infectious, but it was not aimed at me. Their mindless hate and hunger were for the people in the stadium.

And so, I killed with no fear of retaliation.

They were blind and deaf to me.

As they crushed around me moving inward, I struggled to move against them in the opposite direction.

Finally, with a swath of corpses behind me, I made it outside of the stadium.

Overcome by a wash of revulsion, I stood still in the sea of undead, taller than most, and able to see the expansive spread of the horde as it writhed around the stadium.

I was on the wrong side of where I needed to be.

Pressing into the horde, I crushed skulls, shattered faces, and scrambled brains with my hands as I crept along the perimeter of the stadium.

The sun stood high in the sky, and was already sinking toward the western horizon, when I finally saw my goal, the key to my plan.

The other one like me.

I stared at it from amid the flow of zombies. It must have sensed me, because it diverted its attention from the stadium and turned its deadly stare to me.

I saw hate in those eyes. And I felt fear.

My mind went blank staring at the undone, even from so great a distance. Yet, I forced myself to focus. Around me, zombies were still shoving forward, their mass pressing upon itself and the walls of the stadium. Through the noise of the horde, the subtle cracking and popping from the strain on the massive structure was barely audible to my ears. Still, I stared at the other one like me.

It moved toward me.

My mind raced.

Out of nowhere, I realized my idea of a plan was unlikely to succeed. I could speak. I could express my thoughts in words. It seemed unlikely that this creature with its malicious stare was able to speak.

How was I going to ask it to stop?

How could I impress upon it the need to stop the attack?

I stopped. How was it getting the horde to do its bidding?

I lowered my head, breaking eye contact. And I listened.

The chronic murmur of the horde resonated in the air. More faintly, I heard the distant crying out of the people inside the stadium. Hacking and slashing sounds indicated they were still fighting. Even more quiet were the sounds of the pressure on the structure. I singled all the sounds out. There was more. It was low. Like a hum. No, like a growl. Just barely there, but I could hear it.

I looked up at the other undone.

The source of the sound. Somehow, its growl was reverberating through the horde. Somehow, this drove them into their frenzy.

The crashing inward of another door caught my attention. Shifting to watch zombies pour into the hole in the wall where a door had been, I heard the screams of humans who had not retreated to the ramps. Anger filled my mind.

The crush of zombies mowed over the humans. They were not stopping to feed. They moved onward, inward, making room for more to come in behind them.

The horde was being directed. Herded.

I swiveled my head to face the creature. It was nearer to me now. The growl emanating from its throat was clearer. I could feel it reverberating through me, instilling a desire to obey.

It had to stop.

I could not communicate with this creature. Not in the way I needed to. It would take too long. The people in the stadium did not have that long.

Stepping through the zombies, I pushed toward it—as it pushed toward me.

A strange sensation of regret filled my mind. I didn't want to hurt it. I wasn't even sure I could. At least, according to

Dr. Odensea, it was doubtful that we could be hurt or killed.

Still, as the creature came closer and closer, I decided I was going to stop it. Even if it meant I had to rip its head from its body and destroy its throat. I was going to kill it.

We were within arm's length of each other now.

It stared at me; its head cocked to one side. I stared back at it.

Stringy blonde hair ran down one side of its head. The clothes that hung off its skeletal frame were those of a woman. Somehow, a gold band remained on its ring finger. In contrast to all the zombies around us, its flesh was fully intact. And it had the blue tint same as mine. The undone before me was whole, with the same purplish-black veining showing just under its translucent skin.

It stopped moving. The growling stopped. Immediately, all the zombies stopped shuffling forward. They seemed frozen in place.

Instinctively, I braced myself. I knew I was a threat to this creature. And I was certain it knew this as well.

The undone lifted its head, staring at me down its nose. A rough, garbled call emitted from its mouth, and instantly, all the zombies around me turned to face me.

I did not wait.

I threw myself at the creature, fists ramming into its face before it could react. Its nose pushed backward into its brain, but somehow the creature remained standing, its call now shrill. The zombies about us shuffled closer.

With my fist in its nasal cavity while the creature's hands wrapped around my forearms, I felt for its brain. One hand grabbed what I could, while my other hand crashed into the side of its head. I ignored the sounds of snapping bones. The monster was breaking my arms.

I shifted my body, pushing us both to the ground. My hands in its head, I felt down to the top of the spinal cord. Not knowing why, just following a glimmer of a thought in my mind, I wrapped my fingers around the top of the spinal cord and crushed whatever was in my fingers.

The creature went limp.

But it was still making that sound, making the zombies fall on top of me. I could feel them biting my arms, my legs, my neck. While I felt no pain, I knew there would not be much of me left if I didn't hurry.

The creature under me could not move. I had somehow paralyzed it. I pressed upward against the weight of the zombies and crashed my fists into the monster's skull over and over and over. Finally, the screeching stopped. The fires of hate in its eyes burned out.

The zombies stopped biting me. They shifted off me and started ambling about aimlessly.

I lay there, on the other undone. A daze settled over me. An incredible sense of loss overwhelmed my thoughts.

Finally, I sat up and looked down at the creature I killed. Could it regenerate from that mess? I didn't know. But I knew it could not be allowed to, so I got up and dragged it through the zombie horde until I reached the edges of the mass.

When I found a ditch of high, running water, I severed the head from the body. I tossed the corpse into the water and watched it float away. Then, I picked up what was left of the head and wrapped it in some garbage I found nearby.

Finally, I made my way through the zombies and into the stadium. I had to get the head to a fire.

Once inside the stadium, I realized the zombies were back to normal. They were distracted by the dead humans, falling on the bodies, and feeding on them. All other sounds were muted. I heard no more fighting.

When I stopped to listen, I noticed the crackling of a fire that had been burning prior to the attack. There was the shuffle of the zombies who were not feeding. The pressure on the stadium had stopped, as well as the creaking and popping. The structure was safe. And there, high above me, was the quiet murmur of people on the top floor of the stadium.

I looked upward at the glass windows facing inside.

So many faces. I scanned them.

There was Tamra, staring down at me, a look on her face I could not decipher. The doctor, staring not at me, but at the bundle in my hand. Reminded of what I needed to do, I moved toward the fire and threw it in. I watched it burn, down to the broken skull, the shattered face bones. When the bones themselves crumbled in the heat, I turned back toward the windows.

There. There he was. My friend. Michael.

He was safe.

I looked away. No. Not yet. I still had more to do.

Turning my back to the windows, I practiced making the growling sound I heard the other undone make.

The zombies immediately around me stopped what they were doing. They turned to me.

I growled again, constant this time, and began moving out of the stadium. As I approached the gate, I pushed one vehicle after another out of the way. I needed more room. All the while, I kept growling. And I felt the zombies come up behind me.

Finally, I opened the gate and stepped into the field, where the main body of the horde still shuffled about.

Continuing my growl, I walked through the writhing mass of undead.

As one, the horde turned with me.

They followed me as I led them away from the stadium.

Now, Michael would be safe.

EPILOGUE

THE DOCTOR, leading our group, while the woman called Tamra led another, had James stop the caravan for the night. The humans sat around the trailer that the ambulance was pulling and stared at the creature sitting docile in its cage. I stood near them, but not too close.

"If only Adam had come back," Dr. Odensea said to no one in particular.

We had all heard him lament Adam's absence more than once over the past weeks following our trek away from the stadium. The humans had talked a lot about the need to leave the compromised structure before more people were hurt.

James huffed at the doctor's lament over Adam. He might not have missed having Adam around, but many of the other humans did.

I wondered about Adam. I too wondered if he might find us, find me, again someday.

James, however, made it no secret that he hoped he never saw Adam again. It infuriated him that I was still among the human group, and that the changing one in the cage was with us. He huffed, then he shifted his attention to me.

"Sky is growing faster than you thought it would. What's that all about?" he asked the doctor.

I understood a lot more than the humans thought I did. Many of them seemed apprehensive of the supernatural abilities of my kind, like my sudden jump in growth.

The doctor said my growth spurt was because of the genetics unique to the *undone*, as he called us. At first none of the others liked the name Adam gave my kind, but with the doctor's constant use of it, it was gaining traction. He was still fascinated by other undone, and especially of me. More fascinated than scared, at least.

Michael stepped up behind me, a hand gentle on my shoulder. He leaned down and peered at me. His blue eyes like the sky I was named after.

"Sky is another miracle we may never understand," he said. "Isn't that right, Doc?"

"Hmm? Oh. Yes. Quite," responded the doctor, though his attention was on the undone in the cage. "This one is taking a long time to change. I wonder if Adam's initial transition was this long."

I walked over to the cage. It held the second zombie that Adam had captured at the stadium. The one that he had bitten into at the doctor's request.

Already most of its smaller wounds were healing, though the bigger wounds seemed slower to heal. I could smell the difference, though. There was a difference in its eyes. Not just that its eyes were now like mine, shades of purple all the way through the iris and pupil. No, its gaze revealed intelligence, memory, and no more rage and hunger. Maybe we both could learn to talk like Adam had.

I turned to Michael. Reaching up, I took his hand. It was a gesture he liked; I knew. Since Michael's wife was killed in the attack on the stadium, I thought Adam would like it if I helped keep Michael safe.

James continued to glower at me.

"Dammit, Michael, that ain't your kid. Stop treating it like a toddler. One of these days, that thing is going to bite your damn finger off!"

Copying something I saw Michael do once, I stuck my tongue out at James.

Michael laughed.

DEAR READER

Thank you so much for choosing and reading <u>Undone</u>.

I've learned, and continue to learn, from interaction, feedback, and reviews from my publishing team, launch team, and from readers like you.

For that reason, I sincerely ask:

Now that you've read <u>Undone</u>, please take just a moment to leave your honest thoughts about the book in a review, on a social media post, or on my website.

Your thoughts help other readers better determine if they will enjoy this book or not. You also help *me* better understand how this book measures up and gives me an idea of what I am doing right or wrong.

Thank you so much for reading my book!

C. Borden

ABOUT THE AUTHOR

C. Borden writes across many genres, though her favorite genres to write are Christian fiction and fantasy.

The creator of the World of Mythnium, she introduced her readers to Mythnium through Short Stories from Mythnium: Anthology. Then she published her debut novel, Echoes of Dragons, the first book in the Awakenings series.

C. Borden has also written a Christian historical fiction novel, Great Is His Faithfulness, in addition to several stand-alone short stories.

She draws on her life experiences to enhance her active imagination as she writes. When she's not writing and self-publishing, C. Borden is most likely reading, spending time outdoors, or spending time with her loved ones.

To learn more about C. Borden and her writing, you are invited to sign up for her monthly newsletter:

https://bookhip.com/JBMRWXL

Plus, be sure to visit her website for news on upcoming releases and blogs where she shares more about her life as a writer:

www.authorcborden.com

ALSO BY C. BORDEN

World of Mythnium Books

Echoes of Dragons

Awakenings: Book One

A decade after Mythnium's suns eclipse each other, the White Lord's malignant shadow stretches north to Mythos once more. There, he unleashes his secret weapon: a massive dragon long thought to be extinct.

Three groups of travelers set off on separate journeys, drawn toward the elven city of Elmnas and the answers they hope to find within. Along the way, they face strange factions of creatures united against them as the White Lord's influence grows.

As their paths intersect, the travelers face an uncertain new world where echoes of dragons come to life.

Companions of Dragons

Awakenings: Book Two

The dragons' return divides the group as they struggle to adjust to an astonishing truth: a dragon caused the Cataclysm, the disappearance of the dragons, and the upheaval of magic.

Reeling, the companions react in light of the coming war. Orinus and Estryl must breach the wall of storms. What lies beyond could help them master their unique abilities. In Elmnas, Grazina must reconcile helping her friends with staying behind to fulfill her duties as the royal heir. Aldrina musters the courage to confront her birthright. It may mean leaving behind her chosen life. Meanwhile, far to the south, Libitina and her young companion leave Mygras. A deep-rooted call, which they cannot ignore, beckons them northeast.

Applying their knowledge, the companions rush to defend against the White Lord and his forces. Scattered across the world, the allies fear they'll be too late to protect that which they hold dear: Mythnium itself.

Wrath of Dragons

Awakenings: Book Three - Coming December 2024

World of Mythnium Anthologies
Short Stories From Mythnium: Anthology

Gallant warriors. Reluctant royalty. Lost princesses. Rediscovered magic. Vows of vengeance.

In a world still recovering from The Great Cataclysm, elves, humans, and dwarves find themselves pitted against challenges none of them feel ready for. Still, each carries on, seeking to achieve their goals – love, peace, revenge, and discovery.

These stories lay groundwork through immersive character sketches leading up to the events in Echoes of Dragons, the first fantasy novel of Mythnium.

Short Stories From Mythnium: Anthology II

Return to Mythnium, where tree nymphs, rana, mer, pirates, and more add dimension and life to the fantasy realm. Journey with eight new characters who work to overcome hardships in a world interwoven with magic, light, dark, danger, and hope.

These exciting new stories provide a vibrant glimpse into the world of Mythnium. Rediscover the magic of fantasy adventure as you explore with each new character.

Short Stories from Mythnium: Anthology III - coming 2025

World of Mythnium Stand Alone Shorts

Eliviae

She'd settled into a new life, only to have it shattered when the White Lord's forces attacked her home.

Can she come to terms with her painful past and an uncertain future?

Can she find a place to belong?

Felipai

When legendary sea monsters attack and destroy a mer city, the surviving prince finds himself at the mercy of an elven pirate. While the mer prince has lost all hope, his capture revives hope for the pirate captain. But when the pirate ship is attacked by mer raiders, priorities change in an instant and both their lives hang in the balance.

The God-Keeper

Chosen by the gods, whether you want to be or not. How bad can it be?

It is an honor to be chosen to be the next God-Keeper, yet unaspiring Le'am wants no part of it. When his choice is stripped away and all that had been forbidden is now freely given, he finds his life changed forever.

More By C. Borden

Great Is His Faithfulness

Christian / Historical Fiction

Naomi, faithful wife and devoted mother, finds herself in a foreign land surrounded by people who hate and distrust her family simply for being Judaean.

Ruth, a young Moabite woman, marries Naomi's eldest in order for her father to keep a finger on Naomi's family.

Ten years of distrust, heartbreak, and tragedy rob both women of the men they love. With dreams dashed, they return to Ephrathah as widows, expecting to be treated as outcasts. While Naomi harbors bitterness and worry, Ruth embraces hope. She places her trust in Naomi's guidance and her faith in Naomi's God.

<u>Great Is His Faithfulness</u> is a fictional account of the incredible story of Naomi and Ruth, the relationship they shared, and the blessing bestowed on them after everything seemed to be lost.

Bella's Gift

Christian Fiction

When her human discovers her life hangs in the balance, Bella, a loving and loyal house cat does all she can to bring her human comfort.

Will the gift she has been given for herself be enough to help the one she loves?

Bella's Gift is a short story about the companionship between humans and their pets.

Leaving the Hollow

Young Adult / Supernatural

There is magic and fantasy all around us, but have we grown past the point where we can see it?

For two sisters, at the edge of adulthood, magic and fantasy are real. However, life causes changes expected and unexpected, and the growth it takes to handle those changes has real consequences.

This coming of age story, inspired by a region in Northwest Montana, puts a spin on the age old legend of Sasquatch.

Valiance

Christian / Science Fiction

When a rural settlement at the edge of our galaxy faces a threat science cannot explain, Dr. Lau must choose: save herself and keep her secrets, or reveal her truth to save her community.

In the distant future, no one questions the limitations of science and technology. But on Valiance, a planet far from Earth, everything changes when the nightly fog becomes dangerous, people go missing, and those found are comatose.

Dr. Jena Lau is secretly a woman of faith. In a society where religion has been eradicated and is illegal, she grapples with the reality that neither science nor technology can resolve the threat to her community. As she recognizes the evil attacking her home for what it is, she faces a life-altering decision: save herself by keeping her secrets or try to save everyone else by revealing them. As the inexplicable danger within the fog takes more and more of her community, Dr. Lau's forbidden faith in a god long rejected and forgotten pushes her to act.